T0277798

Here was Once the Sea

Rina Garcia Chua
Esther Vincent Xueming
Ann Ang
GUEST EDITORS

Mānoa: A Pacific Journal of International Writing

Editor
Craig Santos Perez

Advisory Board
Kristiana Kahakauwila
Noʻu Revilla
Shawna Yang Ryan
S. Shankar

Corresponding Editors for Asia and the Pacific
CAMBODIA Sharon May, Christophe Macquet, Trent Walker
CHINA Chen Zeping, Karen Gernant, Ming Di
HONG KONG Shirley Geok-lin Lim
INDONESIA John H. McGlynn
JAPAN Leza Lowitz
KOREA Bruce Fulton
NEW ZEALAND AND SOUTH PACIFIC Vilsoni Hereniko, Alexander Mawyer
PACIFIC LATIN AMERICA Noah Perales-Estoesta
PHILIPPINES Alfred A. Yuson
SOUTH ASIA Alok Bhalla, Sukrita Paul Kumar
WESTERN CANADA Trevor Carolan

Founded in 1988 by Robert Shapard and Frank Stewart

Mānoa is published twice a year and is available in print and online for both individuals and institutions. Subscribe at https://www.uhpress.hawaii.edu/title/manoa/. Please visit http://muse.jhu.edu/journals/manoa to browse issues and tables of contents online.

Claims for non-receipt of issues will be honored if claim is made within 180 days of the month of publication. Thereafter, the regular back-issue rate will be charged for replacement. Inquiries are received at uhpjourn@hawaii.edu or by phone at 1-888-UHPRESS or 808-956-8833.

Mānoa gratefully acknowledges the University of Hawaiʻi and the University of Hawaiʻi College of Languages, Linguistics, and Literature.

manoa.hawaii.edu/manoajournal
uhpress.hawaii.edu/title/manoa/
muse.jhu.edu
jstor.org

CONTENTS

Artist Statement on "The Chorus Offering Compliments" #2 (Sembahku yang terakhir kali)

The continuity of cultural values and traditions is inevitably interconnected with encounters, appropriations, impositions, and pushbacks. All these influence all aspects of life in an overlapping manner, by way of sowing metaphorical seeds and growing thoughts, as well as uprooting and planting other thoughts, knowledge, and moralities from different value systems. This is much needed because perceptions about truth and worldview are located in a web of ideological working systems. Many of these became the basis and regulation on which a people has been deemed worthy of the description of "being civilized." In reality, civilization has been read merely from the point of view of those few in power, power over body, and spirit in this world and in the afterlife. A renewed civilization exists on the soils of Java, to be discovered when humans no longer reign supreme over their own selves, nature, and acts of offerings.

Keberlangsungan suatu nilai-nilai budaya dan tradisi tidak akan lepas dari adanya persinggungan, perampasan dan tarik menarik yang akan mempengaruhi seluruh kehidupan menjadi tumpang tindih. Dengan jalan menyemai dan menumbuhkan, mencabut dan menanamkan pokok pikiran, ilmu, moral dan kepercayaan lain dari sebuah nilai yang berbeda. Karena anggapan tentang kebenaran, tatanan hidup, dalam rangkaian sistem kerja ideologis, yang menjadi dasar serta aturan dalam suatu bangsa layak untuk disebut beradab. Kenyataannya peradaban hanya dibaca dari pemegang kekuasaan, kuasa atas jiwa dan raga didunia dan akhirat. Peradaban ini ada di tanah Jawa, ketika manusianya sudah tak lagi berkuasa atas dirinya sendiri, atas alam dan sesembahannya.

RINA GARCIA CHUA, ESTHER VINCENT XUEMING, ANN ANG

Here was Once the Sea: *An Anthology of Southeast Asian Ecowriting*

Introduction

A man touches his head to the earth amid a ravaged land filled with tree stumps. Clad only in a sarong, he is prostrate before the only tree that remains as a small rain falls incessantly and unceasingly. This is either the end or another beginning.

Like our cover art piece "Sembahku yang terakhir kali" or "The Chorus Offering Compliments" by Indonesian artist Setu Legi, *Here was Once the Sea* emerges from a region keenly aware of its own losses and transformations. As our anthology title suggests, Southeast Asia (SEA) harbors long histories and memories in its deepwaters and highlands, along its shorelines, and across jungle ridges. Formed of islets and vast land bodies, the region is separated by the seas, as much as various upriver townships and agricultural communities are interwoven by the rain cycle. At the same time, it is linked by the Pacific Ocean—deepwaters rife with abundance, histories, political tensions, and migrations.

In fact, Chitra Sankaran and Lu Zhengwen in "Ecology and Indigeneity: An Exploration of ASEAN Literatures" position SEA as a space where "strong intersections and cross-pollinations have occurred over several centuries within the region" (2). In our anthology, SEA refers to the constituent nations of the Association of Southeast Asian Nations (ASEAN), namely, Brunei, Cambodia, Indonesia, Laos, Malaysia, Myanmar, Philippines, Singapore, Thailand, and Vietnam, as well as their associated diasporas. Across the centuries, however, the region has been made up of different imaginings: as part of the monsoon belt and co-opted into the Cold War defense front. Bodies of water have created not only the geography, climate, and economy of this area, but they have also linked the socio-historical destinies of its peoples. Yet, the rich and vast cultures within the "Southeast Asian" umbrella are often devolved into tidy homogenous assumptions about its peoples, more-than-human species, and ecological megadiversity—especially in the west, where much environmental scholar-ship is supported and circulated. The burgeoning urgency around the climate discourse in Asia, where the Pacific Rim of Fire sits and rapid glob-alization (plus militarization) is constantly occurring, has created a clamor for responses to the complex social and environmental challenges faced by Southeast Asians within their region and, for some, where migration has taken them. Chi Pham et al. (2) remind us that to holistically recognize "the ecocritical and ecological imagination of the region" is to also embody the "great cultural heterogeneity of the region" and the diversity of the envi-ronmental cultures of its diverse ethnographic groups. There are multiplic-ities within the term "Southeast Asia," just as there are multiplicities in the expression of how creatives have worlded[1] this specific region.

As intimately linked as the region is with water, it is also threatened by it. Amit Prakash in "The Impact of Climate Change in Southeast Asia" asserts that "long coastlines and heavily populated low-lying areas make the region of more than 640 million people one of the most vulnerable to weather extremes and rising sea levels associated with global warming." The long history of resource extraction, colonization, imperial ruin, and neoliberal agendas has ravaged the resource-rich countries of SEA. Despite this visible vulnerability to climate collapse, SEA is still struggling to amplify its voice among the sea of discussions about the environment and our collective futures. Thus, SEA creatives—as evidenced in this volume—have shifted to an urgent, petitional undertone: the stories and voices of SEA deserve *to take up space*.

This anthology represents a chorus of offerings, first and foremost to the land and the sea, and second to you, our readers, as an invitation to attend to the urgencies and travails of our homes. On the one hand, while the anthol-ogy is comprised mostly of anglophone texts, which reflect the aspirations of regional writers to speak across borders and to the globe at large, the English of these pages is inhabited by meanings and associations that make the language our own. This can be seen in the use of indigenous names of plants and places in the works of Annisa Hidayat, Diana Rahim, and Mohamed Shaker, or through rhymes and sounds in the poems of Natalie Foo Mei-Yi and Teresa Mei Chuc. At other times, the native language emerges like weeds, surprising and demanding to be noticed, as in Enbah Nilah's use of Tamil, which persists as linguistic, cultural, and historical memory in a legacy of erasure.

On the other hand, the prevalence of English is also a direct result of col-onization in SEA countries like the Philippines. The USA's one hundred years of rule in the archipelagic nation-state have solidified English as a ver-nacular that interpolates a particular kind of elite education and social class. In relation, E. San Juan contends that because of the hegemonic implications of how English endured as a privileged medium of writing in the Philippines, the choice to write in English is ultimately a political and ethical one (76). It is neither a free choice nor a mere aesthetic decision, he reminds us, yet there is the subaltern's resistance to the hegemony by owning the struggle to fully and wholly express one's self in the colonizer's tongue. This is how we make the language, which oppressed our ancestors in multiple ways, our own. Carmie Ortego's (Waray) and Alvin Yapan's (Tagalog) creative pieces, which are both published in their mother tongue and English, respectively, demonstrate this negotiation between one's native language and culture, as well as both the possibilities and limitations of translation.

When we began work on a proposed volume of ecowriting from SEA, we imagined the region biomaterially as the unwilling recipient of colonization and extractionist developments over the past five hundred years. The rubber plantations of Malaya come to mind, as do the vast sugarcane haciendas of Las Islas Filipinas and the spice trade in the Dutch East Indies. These transformed the ecological and geopolitical landscapes of the region: kingdoms and sultanates centered on ancient mandalas of power became part of a global capitalist economy yoked to western imperial metropolises. World War II ushered in an era of nation-states and borders that compartmentalized SEA into discrete identities and cultures.

Little did we expect to receive writing that would boldly challenge such a narrative. Though we actively sought writing from the constituent states of ASEAN and their associated diasporas, the thirty-seven creative entries and twenty-nine writers in *Here was Once the Sea: An Anthology of Southeast Asian Ecowriting* present a deeply realized vision of SEA as porous and migrational, where the rhythms of humankind and nature-kin are organically intertwined across wet and dry seasons; the upwelling of ocean currents across the archipelago; its highlands and rainforests; paddies and rivers; and the beating hearts of its urban centers; from which travellers issue forth, part of an ever-evolving circuit that bridges the Indian and Pacific Oceans, and cycles through the South China Sea (or the West Philippine Sea). The writers and the people of the region live and remember more profoundly than we know. The poems, fiction, and creative nonfiction in our anthology explore the ecological across a multi-scalar spectrum, featuring both geological landscapes and visceral botanical or animal entanglements, inheriting histories and spiritualities that defy and disrupt modern epistemologies.

The notion of ecowriting in itself, what constitutes environmental writing within the context of SEA today, has dissolved, expanded, and been re-envisioned in the curational process of this body of work. When the anthology was first dreamed into being, we had expected to edit an anthology that would be in the purest sense of the word *ecocentric*, with a strong ecological and environmentalist focus. The idea was seeded in *Making Kin: Ecofeminist Essays from Singapore* and *Sustaining the Archipelago: An Anthology of Philippine Ecopoetry*, motivated by the lack of an ecocentric anthology of creative writing from SEA. However, as we embarked on the process of reading through the submissions, we began to see that the environmental and ecological were very much entangled with the personal, familial, generational, cultural, social, historical, political, and spiritual aspects of the self. These poems, fiction, and creative nonfiction works of ecowriting were themselves intricate ecologies of interbeing, characterized by layers of stories, spiritualities, remembering, and reimaginings as told through a diverse range of contributors from SEA.

It was enlightening to see the expansive and creative responses to the nuances of what constituted an "environment" in SEA from the submissions; in fact, there were many deliberations on which pieces to shortlist and which to keep in view. In the end, the collection brought to life what the original desire was for such an anthology: multivalenced and communal perspectives of the environments and lived experiences that encompass the Southeast Asian region and beyond. The ecological consciousness in the anthology expands beyond the perceptions of what "Southeast Asia" is and becomes a testimony to the interconnectedness of spirituality, myths, Indigenous persistence, and post/colonial histories that have shaped and continue to shape the hybrid identities of this space.

Here was Once the Sea engages with the themes of migrancy and the diaspora in SEA. Our volume explores how hybridity lends itself to a more reflexive, compassionate, ecologically engaged way of imagining one's place on earth; Indigeneity, shamanism, and engaged ecospirituality as a reconciliatory means of reconnecting with and relating to earth and fellow earth others; ecofeminism as defined by an ethos of care, kinmaking, and interspecies kinship where the self *inter-is* with others through an entangled empathy; and queer ecologies and locating gender/queerness in the ecology, where queerness, through its intentions to defamiliarize and destabilize fixed notions, offers readers a way into disintegration, decay, transformation, and rebirth.

The anthology opens with Khairani Barokka's "doa tanah / dirt prayer," where the speaker meets the earth at "ground level," in an act of shared rootedness to the paddy field where the blessing is being made:

> *lower me rooted,*
> *soil-breasted.*
>
> *iridescent, brown,*
> *calm with earthworms.*
>
> *meeting maker at ground level,*
> *lying straight, agog in peat.*

It then moves through the personal, familial, and geographical landscape of hills and mountains, of interspecies kinships as in Christina Yin's "Borneo Reborn," before crossing borders and boundaries of land and sea into diasporic ecoconsciousness and dislocation. Roots, rain, soil, forest, river—these elemental bodies are the recurring motifs that characterize the landscape of SEA, as is the constant search for what it means to be home, even as densely populated and gritty urban landscapes arise and expand across the region. Mark Angeles' "Hut in a Bottle" brings to our attention the transactional ways in which we relate to our Southeast Asian neighbors through tourism and the conflation and commodification of culture. Can we relate to others in a way where all parties involved thrive? This is an ethical and environmental question that the anthology raises.

What have we lost individually and as a collective, and how can we restore our shared losses across the generations? The poetry of Enbah Nilah and Diana Rahim's "The Restoration" excavate the history of the earth to contend with grief, loss, and the longing to plant new seeds of life in the aftermath of death:

When half of that forest was cut down, it felt like she had to grieve another kind of death.

As if she was being denied even the comfort that spatial consistency brings; as if the distance from memory had widened. Now she didn't just have to remember her walks with her daughter, she also had to do the job of remembering the forest. She was twice removed.

Yet, as nature teaches us, all things change, and death and life are connected in an unbroken circle. Natalie Foo Mei-Yi's poem "Clay," from which the title of the anthology is derived, reminds us that, like the earth, we too are mutable and can be transformed, "stroked and kneaded" into shape as long as we remain wet and soft like clay. Here, the anthology flows into the waterway of tsunami warnings and storms in Teresa Mei Chuc's Mekong River. Through storytelling, readers inhabit fictitious worlds where the earth is created anew ("The Belly of the Beast," Gabriela Lee). Like the snake, we shed our skin in the hopes of seeing with clarity and compassion that the thriving of the self is dependent on the thriving of the other ("Clouded Eyes in Paradise," Pamela Ng). Forgetting, remembering, scavenging, decaying, sowing, reaping—the words of Mohamed Shaker, Choo Yi Feng, and Wong Phui Nam lull and calm us, calling us home.

The closing poem "Come Home," by Hmong poet Kevin Yang, traverses continents and seas, leaving and returning home through language. The anthology closes with the couplet: "I am going./ I am going," conjuring an image of spaciousness and endless possibilities. Is the speaker going back home, going away from home, or is the speaker going back home each time they arrive someplace new, since the earth teaches us that we are all her children? In some ways, *Here was Once the Sea* is root, rain, soil, forest, and river. It is also prayer, ritual, death, decay, and rebirth. It asks that we remember the old language of spirit, earth, land, sea, and sky. It is a gift, an offering, a chorus of voices from the peoples, lands, and spirits of

SEA, real and imagined, collective and particular. It is a homecoming to earth, to home, and to self. Come home, reader. We are going, we are going.

Bringing the works into this volume has been a privilege: gifts that wash up upon our shores, offerings from a chorus that stretches from the arms of the Creator and into the lands and seas that have given so much of us life. *Here was Once the Sea* is in many ways the culmination of a collaborative project that brings such compilations to your fingertips or into the bright light of your screen; yet, it is also a beginning. Like how the voices of the chorus persist and resist, this anthology is only the beginning of how we sing our stories. These are the stories we share and the stories we carry in our *pasiking*[2] as we follow movements toward our destinies. These are the stories that sing of hope—for ourselves and for our world—those that we whisper silently to ourselves as we touch our lips to the familiar earth and wait for the incoming monsoon rain to fall gently on our backs, our fields, and our rivers.

NOTES

1. Rob Sean Wilson in the Introduction to *A Geo-Spatiality in Asian and Oceanic Literature and Culture: Worlding Asia in the Anthropocene* cites Ananya Roy and Aihwa Ong to state that worlding in an Asian-specific context can become a "reflective art of being global that takes place without evacuating cultural-political differences that matter" (16).

2. Or knapbasket, a basket backpack commonly found among the Indigenous groups in Northern Luzaon of the Philippines.

WORKS CITED

Pham, Chi, et al. "Bonding ASEAN Together through Literary Studies, Ecological Criticism and the Environmental Humanities." In *Ecologies in Southeast Asian Literatures: Histories, Myths and Societies*, edited by Chi Pham, Chitra Sankaran, and Gurpreet Kaur, 1–8. Wilmington, DE: Vernon Press, 2019.

Prakash, Amit. "The Impact of Climate Change in Southeast Asia." *IMF Finance & Development Magazine*. September 1, 2018. www.imf.org/en/Publications/fandd/issues/2018/09/southeast-asia-climate-change-and-greenhouse-gas-emissions-prakash (Accessed: August 23, 2023).

San Juan, E., Jr. "Philippine Writing in English: Postcolonial Syncretism Versus a Textual Practice of National Liberation." *Ariel: A Review of International English Literature* 22, no. 4 (1991): 69–88.

Sankaran, Chitra, and Lu Zhengwen. "Ecology and Indigeneity: An Exploration of ASEAN Literatures." *The Journal of Ecocriticism* 8, no. 1 (March 2018): 1–4.

Wilson, Rob Sean. "Introduction: Worlding Asia Pacific into Oceania— Worlding Concepts, Tactics, and Transfigurations against the Anthropocene." In *Geo-Spatiality in Asian and Oceanic Literature and Culture: Worlding Asia in the Anthropocene*, edited by Shiuhhuah Serena Chou and Soyoung Kim, 1–31. New York City: Springer International Publishing AG, 2022.

KHAIRANI BAROKKA

doa tanah / dirt prayer

lower me rooted,
soil-breasted.

iridescent, brown,
calm with earthworms.

meeting maker at ground level,
lying straight, agog in peat.

toes wrapped in tender shoots,
shoulders fertile with moonlight.

horizon-wide hips
in paddy field blessing.

rhythmic hands tapping *dry season*
wet season dry season wet—

tomorrow's another warm betting ground,
a place-based faith in no lost state.

legs sludging off a gash of chemicals,
hoping mine-makers weep their blood

for a change. the sunrise a mouth
of glowing clay, greets mineral

selves we are as its own cubs.
caulking our joints

with the love of other bodies,
flesh as rainforest and rice, endless.

WONG PHUI NAM

Into The Vale

He woke up in a valley of farms and slaughterhouses,
wet from the streams that tumbled abundantly
from the base of soaring angsanas upslope.
They cradled an eden of choral insects and birds
nursed by a milky sun. Going down,
he stumbled on bones white as mushrooms
sprouting from the grass. They were pig; they were human.
He was in country that did not care much for its own.
At the farms below, he found breeders
who had appetites for more than the flesh
of their slaughtered pigs, and fed like them
off public troughs. In the scent of blood and terror
on the wind carried from the slaughterhouses,
he heard a distinctly human cry. He was afraid.

Bird Vomit, Vomit Bird

(CW: animal death, emetophobia, parental abuse, implied self harm)

There's something stuck in my mouth. A foreign object that twists and squirms in the warm crevice between my upper gums and cheek is an annoyance. With no water in sight, I strain the muscles of my tongue to get rid of it. I scrounge and scrape until the half-chewed piece enters my gullet without objection.

Urgh.

The stray strand of Bird's Nest slithers down my throat, leaving behind its acrid and saccharine trail. I glance back down at the blue and white porcelain bowl in front of me. The liquid in the Fine China bowl was barely touched. Yellow mucous infested with worms birthed from gelatinous white spit: why would anyone voluntarily drink this?

With the large golden pot of Bird's Nest soup as its centerpiece, the round dining table seating seven feels much smaller, though we are only a family of three. My parents' hands are firmly placed on the table's glass surface while their disdainful stare burns into the top of my head. My gaze remains low, knowing their dark, hollow eyes are seeping with disappointment from my unfilial nature. After all, how could the sole heir to their thriving Bird's Nest harvesting company hate Bird's Nest? The permanent frowns embedded in their faces as they finish their coffee brewed with the burnt sweetness of Bird's Nest essence will serve as my reminder. As long as I'm under their roof, I must drink. The bowl must be licked clean, even if I have to lick it off the floor. Bird's Nest, it's always about Bird's Nest.

I've mustered up the strength, time and time again, to force myself to like it. I even took up smoking, thinking nicotine could mask that nauseating taste; this effluent-infused drink can't even be drowned out by alcohol. Nothing works. My molars grind at the mere thought, clamping my jaw shut against the substance. With just one sip, I can sense the pit of my abdomen running amok and crushing my insides in visceral contractions.

All I can do is pick up the soup spoon to appease them, tapping against the edge of the bowl as I make eddies within the sludge. The white noise gradually distracts them from my insubordination, and their ungrateful child disappears into the gray cement walls of the dining room. Curt business conversations fill the void, and between their exchanges, I could briefly hear the phrase swiftlet apartments. Phantom pains begin welling up at the back of my mouth, while a bittersweet taste permeates it. I can't help but linger in that sordid place—that house, how could I forget?

I was young when they brought me there. When they said we were visiting the birdies, I thought it would be innocuous fun, like a petting zoo.

I didn't know.

It was the first time I swallowed a swiftlet whole.

The edifice was a two-story shop lot erected on the edge of a silent town. Plans for concrete malls and a bustling civilization were discarded here. What remained were the weeds and rusted construction materials. Metal shutters blocked every entrance into the building, and the grated windows on the upper floors were all boarded up with planks or newspapers. Once inside, the cacophony drowned out my senses, until my bones tremored underneath its weight. It was a wailing chorus of pain that fell like a deluge from the ceiling beams above. Hundreds of eyes were illuminated, calling out freedom that can never be attained in the darkness of the dilapidated structure. I found no birdies here, no gentle chirruping—only primal, vicious screeching. This tumultuous noise burrowed deep in my ears and laid eggs that hatched into my nightmares to come.

Yet my parents were unbothered, as if the swiftlets' cries were merely background chatter, and trudged deeper into the back of the building with their flashlight. Even when we arrived at a separate room beyond the swiftlet spit harvesting area, the noise wasn't completely sealed off. The piercing shrieks infiltrated the entire edifice and leaked in through the gaps of the door. Mother cracked open the fridge within the suffocating storage room to find three porcelain bowls wrapped in foggy plastic. The corners of my parents' lips curled into a wide grin as they looked at its contents. My face, however, scrunched up upon witnessing the gelatinous, ruddy liquid. The indiscernible gray globule within the soup merely prompted more questions.

"What's this?"

Father had to stop midway through his drink, replying to me in a low voice and a furrowed brow: "It's Bird's Nest soup. Very good for your health. Now drink."

Hesitation still lurked, but I nodded without a word and peeled open the plastic that shrouded it. The gray thing was wrinkled and shaped like a deformed clay ball. My body froze, realizing what those bulging black beads and sharp, obtruding bones were. An infant swiftlet's body was half submerged in my soup.

I screamed at my parents for help, but Mother merely tutted and pried open my mouth. She shoved the bowl's edge toward my unwilling maw, and the chilled soup dribbled down my chin. The viscous texture of the dead bird pressed against my upper lip, and its carrion stench became most palpable then. I could no longer resist, my mouth parting for just a moment to breathe.

Gulp.

Down my orifice it went. The congealed blood stewed in the soup engulfed my taste buds with a metallic sweetness. My adolescent throat could barely fit the carcass as its undeveloped wings and beak gouged at the walls of my oesophagus. I could feel it almost wriggle back to life. It carved its path deep within my organs to its own grave. My mind refuses to let go of that feeling—the sensation of putrid, raw flesh bulging against my trachea. Every encounter I have with that wretched Bird's Nest soup will always end the same way. Tonight is no different.

I flee to the washroom, despite the displeased looks I glimpse through my bleary sight. The toilet relieves me of my suffering as I cling to its sides and plunge my face into its bowl. The dry heaving starts first. Then, from the hackling, a pale-yellow amalgamation made from chunks of undigested meals and bitter bile rises to the surface. My stomach fumes at the need to purge the vileness it has held onto, but the vomit sputters like a fountain with a clogged spout. Something is stuck in my throat.

Tears now fall from my face while I strangle my throat into submission with palms pressed against my pharynx. When my violent coughing sent it splashing into the toilet water below, I thought my vomiting fit was done. Yet in the haze of exhaustion and the humidity of the closed space, harrowing chirps fill the room. My eardrums are hammered by the incessant avian cries until even the sound of my own heart is lost.

"Chee. Chee. Chee. How could you? Waste my flesh. You swallowed me. Chee. Chee. Chee."

The shape of a gray bird fetus reveals itself in the yellow substance. My tongue recoils as it tastes the blood and slime. My entire mouth is coated with that awful sweet sensation along with bitter bile. No matter how much I retch and how desperately I want to sink my nails into the flesh of my tongue to claw it out, I can still feel the bird's bare skin sliding about my throat. Before yet another paroxysm of vomiting, I ran down the flush handle until all traces of it were gone in the whirlpool.

Shaken, my feet manage to drag me out of the toilet. But in my absence, the number of bowls on the dining table multiplied. A glimpse of my parents indulging in their second bowl of that drink was all it took for me to relapse. There's nothing left for me to puke as I shrivel into a ball on the marble floor. All that releases from my dry lips is drool. My panic attacks are usually nothing to them, yet for the first time, I could sense the shadow of their figures looming over me.

"Look at your saliva! Like Bird's Nest!" Father exclaims in delight. My entire body convulses in gut-wrenching disgust, feeling my drool harden next to my face. My fingers are the first to react, reaching into the inside of my mouth to mutilate my tongue with whatever strength I possess. But the two older adults stopped me before I could damage anything and dragged me to my room on the first floor.

"Quickly! We need to put this in a dark room! For more saliva production!"

"What a fortune we will make! Premium Human's Nest soup! Useful for once!"

"We expect you to fill that bucket by morning."

My depleting cigarette lighter, which I had kept in my pocket, provides a paltry light in the tenebrous space. But I find no comfort from its weak flame in my teary-eyed state. Even as my fists tremble and bang against the door, my parents show no sympathy. What else could my shivering form do? Besides spew spit into the pail until my mouth cracked and bled from dehydration. In spite of all that effort and sobbing, it didn't even reach the halfway mark. The rotten fetor from the bucket worsens the longer I'm trapped. The inescapable odor of spoiled eggs left to fester for what seems like years provokes my gag reflex. But with nothing to throw up, my body remains in that perennial loop of hurling and loathing the odor of stomach acid mixed with saliva.

Fatigue takes over as I cling to consciousness. I don't want to feel my own saliva spilling out of my mouth anymore. Or to experience that repulsive syrupy soup again. I yearn for bland water that won't have the tang of my own regurgitation. Freedom—that's what I would like to taste. Is it so wrong to desire the sides of my lips to stop burning from my puking and for my teeth to feel clean and unstained by my own oesophageal acid? All I want is a scorching sensation that will quell the agony in my throat, a flame that will glaze my mouth and desiccate those abhorrent flavors.

One lighter. One blaze.

Freedom at the tip of my tongue.

Saola

You come to me in dreams
from my Motherland
emerging from the forest
your horns like black swords

How many wars have you survived?

How I try to live like you
evading hunters who are
always in search of me.

Rhinoceros

"At 45, Sudan was an elderly rhino, and his death was not unexpected. Hunted to near-extinction, just two northern white rhinos now remain: Najin, Sudan's daughter, and Fatu, his granddaughter, both at the conservancy."
—*The New York Times* (March 20, 2018)

"About 709,000 years ago, someone butchered a rhinoceros using stone tools on the Philippine island of Luzon. That may not seem remarkable—except that humans weren't supposed to be in the Philippines so long ago."
—*CNN Philippines* (May 2, 2018)

i.
The last white rhino sways
even when no one
is looking.
Its curves biologists and sculptors
will someday agree feel right.
Its hooves, horns,
massive wholeness
strangely at peace with the earth—
blades of grass bow in its wake.

ii.
Long before our desire for worship
and things that comfortably fit
in the palm of a hand,
hunger took hold of everything,
made for the wildest
of pairings: man to animal,
stone axe to marrow,
teeth to flesh,
river water to fire,

horn ash to magic.
The odd-toed ungulate
did not stand a chance.
Nothing, no one, ever did.
Thousands of years later,
the absence of fossils
still tell the same story.

iii.
The peopling of the islands
begins and ends with a set of tools,
mismatched artifacts,
and days will continue to claim
what is never ours to begin with
no matter the marks we make:
caves swallow men and women,
skies bless and ravage
in equal measure,
animals ever the master.
There is not enough discovery
in the future to patch up what is gone:
We are all bones, histories
just waiting to happen.

Mother Tongue

They see each other first in the last of the day's light. He is still new to the land, only three weeks out of Johor, where he had been born and raised, trained in the jungles in the north of the state in preparation for his arrival here, and flung out to this kampung in the foothills of a vast country, the sky wide and flat above him, the fields of padi an endless ripple. The snatches of mist make the air thin and cold. Especially when the evening comes.

This is when he sees her first; this is when she sees him first. She is coming up the dirt path, a bag swinging at her side. He cannot tell what is inside, but it doesn't matter. There is the last of the day's light glinting in her hair, against her collarbone, a spark. He is standing against the sun, and so he himself is almost eclipsed by it; she notices this. Then there is a sound that she recognizes but that is new to this place—the azan for maghrib rupturing the air between them and around them. This jolts him; he turns from her, following its sound back toward the barracks behind him, toward their makeshift masjid. But he does look back once, and she too is looking at him. She does not lower her eyes.

It is 1963, and somewhere in a teak-paneled boardroom, men are wearing Western dress and speaking in the English they perfected in the halls of Oxford and Cambridge, using that same English to espouse the Asian nationalism that has risen its head. There are plans being made to cobble together a nation. That is why he is here. A man from Johor sent over the South China Sea, crossing all that blue and disembarking on the port of Jesselton, houses on stilts above that endless water, the rise and fall of mountains in the distance. His first sight of that large island called Borneo; he is in its north. The language around him is foreign; he feels as if he should know it, but at the same time, it always rattles him and wrong-foots him. And the Malay that he hears is slower than he is used to, like a drawn-out song.

A month before this he had said goodbye to his family in the south of Johor, had been put on a train and sent to the north of the state, been thrust into jungle. The rumor was the threat of the archipelago, of Sukarno's ire. *Indonesia surrounds us, these are the points where she might come through. Johor, of course, so close to Riau. And North Borneo and Sarawak, through*

Kalimantan. We have ample men here; you, we will send east. The idea was that an invasion, if it came, would be through the jungle. Through the gnarl and the dark. The fighting would be tight, hand-to-hand. Intimate. He had been born just before the war itself but he was of course familiar with how the Japanese had come down on bicycle; nothing as brash as a tank could have grappled with the landscape and won.

Either way, he had trained for a month in Kota Tinggi, his head heat-addled and thick with the music of insects and the rustle of leaves and wind, with the myriad light that skipped from surface to surface before disappearing completely, folded into the black womb of the earth. And then he was brought away from everything he knew, plunked onto the fringe of this kampung in the north of Borneo in preparation for who-knows-what, his hands tight and cold because they are at the foothills of a mountain range, mountains taller than he has ever seen in his life, the sight of them blue and far off in the distance, their peaks obscured by cloud. Three weeks he has spent here, and the people of the kampung have been wary of them; not quite afraid but mistrusting, he could hear it in the way they spoke and the way they held themselves as they walked past him. Past the rest of his brothers. Were these really to be his countrymen? The imam they had brought with them then one night sat them down and said, *this cannot go on. Let us make our rounds, let us say our welcome. All we have to do is speak to one another, kan? That's all.*

And so that was what they had done. They had knocked tentatively; doors had been opened with equal hesitation. What were the people of the kampung to do with these young men from the peninsula, who could neither eat pork nor drink their rice wine? Who thus could not engage in their merry-making, in their heightened song and dance that, through the long night, would turn lonesome and sad, even with a crowd? But they had let them in, and they had become familiar with each other. They shared a language after all, a history. A possible future. And there was the threat of Indonesia hanging around them; that brought them together. *What is it like where you come from?* A man about his age had asked him one evening, both of them hanging around for a smoke. For a moment, he had paused, the cigarette alighting between his fingers. The rustle of the jungle around them. The sea to the east. He had come from a fishing village, and his skin still had that sungleam and saltgleam. *It's not like this*, he said, *but it's not that different, also.*

The next time she sees him, she is working at the neighboring town's kedai. She sees a darkening at the entrance and looks up. This time she looks away the moment their eyes meet and has to feel his presence instead—sense him walking through the aisles, looking for something. The owners of the shop are Chinese, and behind her is the ancestral shrine, the glow of red and varnish, and the powdery choke of incense. Her fingers rise to the crucifix that lies against her throat, and *now* she looks up. He is standing by the shelf of sweets, just looking at them, and she cannot help it; she has to speak.

"You are looking for what?"

He turns to look at her, and their eyes meet again. It is ridiculous, but that feeling she has when she looks at him—that feeling she had that first moment on the path. Pure instinct in her throat.

He grabs something off the shelf and comes toward her. He has a tube of sour plum candy in his hand that he puts down on the counter.

"My mother likes this," he said.

"Your mother is here, too?"

"No."

She takes his money and gives him his change. She takes care not to touch his skin—with anyone else, she would have been mindless, but she cannot do this now; something stops her. She is acutely aware of where her body ends and his begins.

He lingers at the counter and then looks up at her. His eyes were first on the crucifix around her neck, then into her own eyes. Then someone else enters, and the moment breaks. He mumbles *thank you* and leaves. She puts her right hand on her left wrist after he goes. The skin there is hot, almost feverish. It is absurd, but she cannot help it; the skin by her neck is warm too, beneath the crucifix, which itself is a stain of heat against the bone.

It is inevitable that one night, one of the doors he knocks on is hers. They have just sat down for dinner, her aunt, uncle, and cousins, and they have just said the prayers, her aunt giving thanks to Kinoingan, making the sign of the Cross, and their murmur of *Yesus Kristus*. Then they knock on the door.

"It's the fellas from Semenanjung," one of her cousin says.

"What do they think, they're going to eat with us?"

"We have to invite them in either way, isn't it?"

"It's fish and vegetables and rice only."

"Bah, better than pork. They're circumcised—"

She leaves their babble, nods at her uncle, and rises to open the door. She is prepared to see him, and when she opens the door to his face, to the night unfurling behind him, she understands that something has shifted between them; she can feel it in her spine, which allows her to look him in the eyes the way she had done on that first day. Without hesitation. Like a blade of light in a dark room.

But he is not alone, and there are introductions to be made, with the rest of the family coming out onto the verandah. The soldiers have brought fruits, things that everyone can eat, and fistfuls of chili. He is holding a line of salted fish, and it is this he presents to her that she takes from him, her head inclined in thanks. And then, because she feels brave, she moves her fingers so that they brush against his, and he does not move his own hand away, and for a moment they stand there. It is cold on the verandah, and in the distance, the mist has risen, obscuring the path, the dark jungle beyond, the deepening sky, and the frenetic hum of the trees at night. The strange pulse of light that he had become familiar with during his own month within. But she is standing now, next to him, and behind them is the oily glow of the kerosene lamp and the smell of fried fish and belacan. It reminds him of home.

Her uncle is welcoming them in.

"Come," he is saying. "You cannot drink but you can eat with us, you have brought all this, thank you. Come in, come, eat."

She breaks the touch between them and turns to enter the house. But then she looks back at him and smiles, and all that heat between them breaks also, her entire face changing, the glint of light at her neck in her eyes too, and he is frozen in time even after she leaves, until he realizes that he is left there, standing alone, in the dark of the night. Then he gathers himself and enters the house.

They meet in secret, in shadow. The kampung and town are only so small, but there is a world that unfurls beyond them, in the shadow of a tree or by a river. Once in a room above the shop with everyone out, and the mournful wail of some singer from Hong Kong coming through the thin wooden wall. Turning to the window, they could see the mountain's rise and fall out of the spine of the earth. There is no longevity here, no future for them. He cannot be here forever; he is only here because of the threat of violence, because of the machinations of men in boardrooms. First on a frigid island in Europe with the desire for timber and tin, rubber and rattan, spice and silk; now discussing the making and unmaking of a nation that wants to throw off the last chains of Europe. And then there is the question of worship. He had once put his thumb against her crucifix without thinking and had later felt its imprint against his skin. *I stole this from a priest*, she had murmured. *He had taken my grandmother's drums.* And he himself looking from left to right in prayer, the gestures they have brought with them from the peninsula, the voice of the imam from Perak, thinking of her, of the feel of her hair in his hands like water, the bone beneath the skin—there is no longevity for them; there is no future. Only a single moment in a darkened room or with the perfume of the earth around them. She pushes his hair away from his forehead and breathes his name into his scalp, holding it in her mouth very briefly before the release. This country that they have made their own.

It is night when it comes, of course. The sky heavy with darkness.

Movement, a voice says through the transmission, its crackle. *Sukarno is feeling bold tonight.*

Immediately and quietly, they spring into action. Gathering their things and putting on their clothes. They enter the jungle, slipping through the silence of the night. The kampung is asleep and the town is asleep. Only the dogs were beneath the houses, their eyes gleaming in the dark.

Around him is the glimmer of the earth. The weight of the air between the trees. What ghosts, he wonders, lurk here? Whose spirits? The other day, he had passed by the church during mass and heard the language of their worship—her mother tongue, one that he could not understand. A language to him like a chorus of rivers. She was somewhere inside that low-roofed building, her hands moving in prayer. *Always I have wanted to know— you eat your God?* He had asked. She had replied—*her body is rice; his body is bread.* Ya' Allah. The thought of her even now. He concentrates on the world around him. What if the Indonesians really are here tonight? They would know the jungle as well as them; when they speak, their language will be the same, with only rhythm separating them. Only a ship that arrived sooner or later.

They hold their position; they have hidden themselves between the trees. They will wait until the morning. They have learned to read the jungle-like language and to decipher her like a lover. So that each rustle he feels in his head, so that each shift of light he feels in his veins. A heat between his eyes; the weight of fever. They wait all night, but no one comes. Nothing disturbs them. Strangely, not even a natural sound—all silence. When the morning comes, they return to their barracks. The imam is already packing up his things. They have missed Fajr; they heard the fading notes of that prayer as they emerged from the jungle. He moves through the air as if it was thick water. He wants to sleep for a thousand years.

Two evenings later, they are sitting together by the river. Her hair is loose down her back. They are still in the shadow of the mountain; the mist is creeping up on them. They can smell the sharpness of the water, its hidden metal.

"Will you leave with me?" He asks, and she looks at him.

"Will you stay for me?"

He does not reply, and she looks away and touches her fingers to her crucifix. In the morning, he will leave for a military rotation. She thinks of this place that he had come from—*Johor,* she says to herself, very softly, not wanting him to hear. She is filled with desire then, not just for him, as he is now here in front of her, but for his geography and his history. The country that he has come from, the line of men and women out of which he has come: their spangled music in his blood. All this she wants now to take, even if he is leaving tomorrow itself, even if she will never see him again. And she also wants to give him everything. All that she has, all that she has come from.

"I want to tell you something," she says. "When I was small, my father went into the jungle with my brother. They were looking for something for us to eat. The harvest was bad that year. They should not have gone in; there was bad birdsong in the trees that day—a warning. But we were hungry. In the jungle, my father saw a mouse deer. He was a skilled hunter, his aim was always true. So he shot the mouse deer; he hit its heart, saw it fall to the earth. It made no sound—nothing. All was very quiet, my father said. And then, when he went toward it, he saw that it was my brother he had shot."

He says nothing, and she herself has nothing left to say. She puts her forehead in her hands; she wants to cry; she feels it in her chest, behind her eyes, but nothing comes out. Her shoulders are shaking, but nothing comes out. It is then that she feels his palm on her back, and it is only then that she can finally weep. For how long they sit together like that, she does not know. And he, with her back against his chest and her head beneath his chin, decides against keeping the time. It does not matter what time he returns, what prayers he misses, or what punishments he will gather for being late for his return to the barracks. He will do everything for this.

The sky grows darker. The mist rises, and the black of the sky is broken by the darker darkness of the jungle and the mountains beyond them. The silence of the starlight above. For hours, he holds her; for hours, she is held by him. Until all sense of ending and beginning is lost, until they can no longer tell where they end and the earth begins, when it is time to go, they walk in silence, close together, but they do not touch. He sees her off at her house, which is already dark. He puts a hand on her left wrist, and she touches it with her fingertips. He waits while she climbs the stairs to the verandah, until she opens the door. At the doorway, she pauses and looks back. Then she goes through, and he is left alone in the darkness. In the morning, he will leave and board a ship that will take him back south. He waits for a moment in the darkness alone, the wind crisp around him. Then he turns and heads back up the road.

Finding Faults and Dragons_____

A silver dragon washed up on shore just days before the devastation. No one knew what it was—if it was a he, a she, or a god. All they could tell was that it would've measured longer than two fishermen combined, and it was dead.

The dragon's body was limp and cold as it lay among the rocks, its unusually large eyes eternally open and its once scarlet fin gone muddied. A hole under its mouth began to stretch, leaking the being's gray innards onto the sand and ripping its head away from its body as soon as the men held it up for a photo. It took five fishermen to lift it, outstretched. As they gripped the sides of the dragon, they understood it didn't naturally fall from the sky or float up from the shallow waters of Carmen. It was a creature from the deepest depths of the sea—a baby lost, stranded far from home. No one had yet considered it to be an omen.

Two days later, on February 10, 2017, a 6.7-magnitude earthquake struck the nearby Surigao City. With all hands on deck, the Philippine government began assessing the damage. The National Disaster Risk Reduction and Management Council reported that the tectonic event caused at least eight deaths and over two hundred injuries, while the Department of Social Welfare and Development found that the disaster had displaced thousands of families. If they hadn't been directly affected by the earthquake, they hesitated to return home for fear of aftershocks.

Between the 8th and 18th of February, more dragons began appearing on Mindanao shores, either dead or dying. From far away, one could almost mistake them for construction debris or tangled plastic bags. The dragons failed to breathe fire or spin circles in the water; they lay on the ground, their appearance enough to grow concern among residents.

On the 5th of March, the people experienced yet another earthquake: a 5.9-magnitude tremor in Surigao del Norte province, causing at least one death and countless more injuries and displacements. By then, residents of the region began making the connection between the dragons and the disasters. It was a connection others had made centuries before.

- - -

As my mother drove me to school, she pointed at the scene outside her window, at the uneven land just off the highway. "That's a fault," she said. "When the Big One hits, we better not be near here."

All the news outlets had been reporting on the "Big One," the major earthquake that would inevitably hit Metro Manila and cause unimaginable destruction. Though scientists couldn't determine exactly when it would hit, they predicted it could happen in my generation's lifetime.

A driver honked his horn behind our car as my mother navigated the expressway. She always drove slowly, no matter how late I was for class or how crucial her presence was at a meeting, especially when Furball and I were in the car with her.

"Look over there," she instructed me. "The West Valley Fault runs through several of the Valle Verde villages. Even the mansions of White Plains and Green Meadows in Quezon City wouldn't be spared."

I nodded as she explained the ins and outs of fault lines, earthquakes, and beliefs as written in the Boxer Codex. I was thinking about my math exam scheduled for that afternoon.

Furball and I sat in the back of my mother's SUV as I fed him cat food in his crate. My mother called the passenger seat the "death seat," forbidding anyone from sitting beside her unless they accepted the risk of taking the brunt of impact in case of an accident. Instead of being occupied by a passenger, the seat beside my mother was hidden under a growing mountain of what she considered necessities—everything from tissue to canned goods to tin snips.

My mother's car was her war machine—the bunker we could count on if the worst ever happened. But even she seemed terrified of what science had deemed inevitable.

- - -

As word spread about the rise of the dragons and the earthquakes that followed, experts came forward to identify the creatures as oarfish. They were neither mythical nor godly; they were real. The sea serpents were known to live in tropical and temperate waters, as deep as 3,000 feet into the ocean.

Though the people finally had a name for these harbingers of disaster, the oarfish were just as feared as they were before the revelation. A dead oarfish meant trouble brewing at the center of the earth. Beached oarfish became newsworthy instead of just disposable; their movements became a warning to be taken seriously.

The deep-sea fish seemed to have already had a reputation before dying on Philippine shores. A bigger picture began to emerge of these knowing creatures feeling the faults in the waters, reading them for danger all across the world, and passing away in the process.

In Palau, the oarfish is known as the "rooster fish." In many countries, it's known as "the king of the herring." In Japan, the oarfish is called

"Ryugu No Tsukai," or "messenger from the Sea God's palace." Seeing them is equivalent to being given a message to flee or, if left with no other option, prepare. A few years before the Surigao earthquakes, over a dozen oarfish surfaced in Japan. Soon after, in 2010, Haiti experienced a 7.0-magnitude earthquake, Chile an 8.8-magnitude earthquake, and Taiwan a 6.3-magnitude earthquake. In 2011, a 9.1-magnitude earthquake hit Fukushima, causing a tsunami that triggered a meltdown at the prefecture's nuclear power plant and claimed thousands of lives.

Around the same time, oarfish were discovered on the shores of California, a state widely known as an earthquake hotspot due to the San Andreas fault system, where the North American and Pacific tectonic plates collide. In 2020, at the start of a new decade, the discovery of an oarfish in Mexico and the following 7.4-magnitude earthquake in Oaxaca stirred up new fears about the long, silvery creatures.

It seemed the dragons from Surigao were everywhere and nowhere at once. Sightings of them alive were rare, but people would have rather not seen them at all.

Some scientists and institutions are quick to dismiss the oarfish beliefs as mere superstitions, yet others believe it possible that modern-day dragons are especially sensitive to underwater fault movements, their surfacing and eventual deaths being the result of an inability to handle the unexpected pressure changes in the deep sea.

- - -

In my junior year at university, the entire school participated in the Metro Manila Shake Drill. Complete with a hashtag to popularize the exercise (#MMShakeDrill) and Metropolitan Manila Development Authority officers overseeing our adherence to protocol, the drill was held across the metro to prepare us for the possibility of a 7.2-magnitude earthquake along the West Valley Fault.

"Duck! Cover! Hold!" the drill officers yelled on their megaphones. Then, when all was silent, they shouted, "Evacuate!"

Flurries of students rushed to the nearest open spaces, but as they knew it was just a drill, they rushed with no sense of urgency.

As a girl in front of me brisk-walked, she said to no one in particular, "They say it happens every 400 years."

"So what?" one of my classmates asked.

"It's bound to happen again soon."

What no one told us was that the last major earthquake linked to the West Valley Fault occurred around 1645. The girl was right; we were almost at the 400-year mark. The whole reason we were practicing how to survive was the possibility of the "Big One"—the worst-case scenario related to the 100-kilometer fault.

The mere length of the fault gave rise to the possibility of an earthquake of higher magnitude and longer duration than any earthquake previously recorded in the metro, which meant it would claim thousands more lives and cause even worse destruction than could be predicted.

The expressway my mother took every day and the villages we passed would collapse, break apart, or succumb to fire and complete horror. The ground would not only shake; it would fall beneath and around us.

This was enough for me to begin listening to my mother.

- - -

The scientists say the dragons aren't supposed to be silver. In the comfort of the deep-sea darkness, they shine bright red, blue, and even purple. As they float to the surface, they lose color, their vibrancy giving way to paleness.

Though oarfish have grown a reputation for their sheer length, in the waters, they stand tall. They position themselves vertically for protection and for feeding, with their ribbon-like fins shimmering like sequined frills in dim light. One can only imagine how much more frightening they would be if they could thrive along shallow shores. Their bodies, once found, are useless to fishermen, who can neither sell the strange oarfish meat nor profit from them as lab specimens. Much has already been learned about dead oarfish. What scientists lack is information about them.

The oarfish is just one of several deep-sea creatures that make the news as dead omens. Large, heavy sunfish and globsters (unidentified masses) have also been known to strike fear among coastal towns, believed to be messages of caution from down below.

The general consensus, however, seems to be that whatever is bringing typically hidden sea creatures to the surface couldn't be anything to be happy about. The terms "pollution," "global warming," and "climate change" have been thrown around alongside all the myth, but that's all that happens; they stay up in the air.

- - -

"They found another oarfish in the province the other day," my mother told me.

She was driving on the same expressway; it felt like we had had this conversation a thousand times before.

My mind was flooded with images of the metro post-disaster.

If the #MMShakeDrill turned out to be all for naught and everything vanished into ash, survivors would either be fleeing to safer shores or subjected to government force in an effort to prevent or end economic paralysis. Relief operations could last months, if not years, for the humans, for their animal companions, and for the towns whose histories will have been lost to the deep crevices of the earth's crust.

I thought about Furball and how he would handle the chaos, and if I would be alive to provide him with comfort and care.

I pictured the oarfish, unaware of the superstitions and myths surrounding its dragon-like status on land, struggling to survive only inches from the surface of the sea. Perhaps the oarfish have their own beliefs, of journeys upward leading to certain death or of survival as they flee from destruction back home.

Perhaps they, too, are terrified.

I looked back at my mother and asked her, "Was it still alive?"

Mother Body

My *Ibu* is a protector
And her *Ibu* yells across the ocean
to ensure her protection

My mother's freedom
Sewed on
every thread sings a hymn

Her body belonging to money
at risk like pressed metal
on collarbone that flesh prey on

Industrious like *Ama's* hands
Old enough to tell a story of
crying laborers burning their home

Palm and coconut set aflame
their wallets made of cows
that they believed were once God

Permission to change
Yet the Earth is mad
Mad enough to birth billionaires

Batulayar Hill

West Lombok, 2022

villa saraswati of batulayar[1] hill at dusk
I caught the golden ocean light of the sunset
from the graceful villa terrace
the road of the bawah village[2] is very small and long
like an ant trail shrouded in the evening mist;
soft and grey among the sparkling stars
bright moon on a cold evening
the hillside gets warm

some days it rains
villagers without land titles were evicted
the houses shrouded in fog were empty
the wall was destroyed not by the storm
but annihilated

cloudy morning, there is another execution
police sirens and bulldozers roared through the air
down to the serene sea of senggigi[3]
from a distance, among foreign tourists
the hill is the face of a wounded woman

NOTES
1. Batulayar is the name of a tourist centre village on Lombok Island.
2. Bawah Village is a village on Batulayar hill that has experienced evictions.
3. Senggigi is the most famous beach in Batulayar.

Hoang Lien Son Mountains

Uncle pointed at the mountain range
in the distance. He said, "Hoang Lien Son Mountains."
It was so green and beautiful like an emerald.

I heard of that name before, from my father.
Hoang Lien Son Mountains was where he was imprisoned
in a Viet Cong "re-education" camp for nine years.

But this poem is not about the prison camp
or the suffering of my father and the other prisoners
—that is another poem.

In these mountains are critically endangered
western black crested gibbons who live and eat
in the trees, swinging from branch to branch.

The gibbons talk to each other in a language
that my father listened to for nearly a decade.
At dawn, a chorus of howls,
almost birdlike chirps and whistles.
While hanging from a trunk,
a gibbon reaches her hand to scoop up
water from a stream and drinks.

These mountains are a sacred home
to the few remaining species of gibbons,
primates like us.

And when I visited Con Son Island,
I wondered why there was so much pain
in a beautiful place. How much could
humans take without giving back?

CARMIE ORTEGO

*Those Who Dwell in the Wilderness*_____

"SO you're from Talalora? I thought there are a lot of barangan in your town?"

I have been asked this question many times that I have lost count already.

And my answer is always, "Yes. A long time ago." Or, "Not anymore." Or, "They died out."

Different words for the same meaning: it's gone.

But that is our identifier. If you look it up on the Internet, "Talalora" and "barang" always go together. In other words, we are a "haven of faith healers," as a Philippine News Agency article said. That was what we were before, when most people still believed in woodland and sea spirits. Now, that belief only comes back in times of peril.

FIRST lesson in living with the world: *Don't harm animals, especially the little ones, because they don't do you any harm.*

Of course, this doesn't include cockroaches, mice, centipedes, and other house pests. This is only for the lizards, the beetles, the house snakes, and other animals who might only be a little off course. We let them go home, and if the house is already shuttered, we open the exits. Sometimes through the doors, or the windows, or in between the slats of our wooden floor in our old living room. We also try not to touch other animals in the belief that they might be some panalipdanan: a kind of disguise by a magical creature such as a witch or wakwak.

Plants and trees are included in this reminder. Except for the grass, herbs like gatás-gatás (*Euphorbia hirta*), herba buena (*Mentha spicata*), and others shouldn't be plucked. If trees are to be felled, it is the tambalan, or folk healer, who leads the ceremonies, or "whispers hope" while asking permission from the tree. One couldn't just take anything.

When we were young, we were not even allowed to play in grassy areas or those near trees because we might get rowdy and wake those-not-like-us who were sleeping. If home was too far, we needed to ask permission again and say "tabi-tabi" before peeing near the tree. One had to be very respectful, especially of the trees, to avoid darahug or getting sick or possessed.

Humans could also make enchantments to hurt others, and this is where Talalora's identifier as barangan came from. Nay Polen, Nanay's aunt, says, "Talalora was famous for barang palakad; it was all here."

If you were a victim of barang palakad, that meant that you walked over an area in which someone had performed an oracion (chants or prayers usually in a mix of Latin and Waray); that's why you get sick suddenly or in some other kind of accident.

You could also be poisoned, especially if you were careless when eating during the patron or fiesta. It could make you sick for up to three days, especially if the poison seeps into meat. This is also why, when we sang as choir members in our parish priest's barangay masses, we often brought our own drinking water.

In the olden days, the power of the himangnoan, those who knew how to perform enchantments, was very potent. Nay Polen says, "… people in those times, Tatay said, would be instantly afflicted with just a point of a finger," and your nose could be chipped like Apoy Banô. Unlike the rituals shown on TV, which still need hair or a voodoo doll to stick needles in. There was also an oracion that could be chanted for invisibility, which was very helpful during the Japanese times when life was hard.

IF you look at the map, there are only five island municipalities in Samar: Tagapul-an, Almagro, Sto. Niño, Daram, and Zumarraga. Talalora is only considered practically an island because the only means of travel to Catbalogan or Tacloban is through a pump boat. Since 2017, the woman governor had already been seeking funds for the Php 1.1 billion access road from Villareal town to ours for easier travel especially when the seas are rough during bad weather.

If we're going to talk about roads and other infrastructure, there are already funds.

Php 14.1 million access road from Poblacion Dos to Tulac toward the Villareal route to the east, but the budget was not yet released by the Department of Budget and Management (DBM) in 2017.

Php 4.4 million road toward the Tacloban route to the south, linking barangay Placer to barangay Malaguining, the farthest barrio and one of the geographically isolated and disadvantaged areas in Eastern Visayas, according to the 2020 report by the Department of Health. From Placer, it is easier to travel to the Poblacion because the road well worn by students who use it when the seas are rough is now concretized. This was how my aunt would go home on foot for more than an hour after teaching, especially if it was low tide in Placer because it was further inland and not a natural port. Boats to and from the barangay would even go one at a time because the channel toward the port was too narrow.

Php 5.4 million was released by the DBM for our evacuation center in Poblacion Dos. This is after the 2016 governance assessment report, which asserted that we did not pass the criteria for disaster preparedness and environmental management. There are already pictures on the website of the Department of the Interior and Local Government showing that there are steel bars erected at the proposed site, but even the municipal accountant's report also says that construction has not started.

These are the findings of the 2018 Fisheries Compliance Audit:

We don't have a 10% area limit of aquaculture such as fish farming.
We don't have a 15% area for fishery reserves.
We don't have a limit for fishery activities such as the use of closed season.
We don't even have a representative from the fisherfolk.
There are fishery sanctuaries and catch ceiling limitations, yes.
But there is also unauthorized fishing.
Fishing through explosives like dynamite.
Coral exploitation and exportation.
Fishing using a fine mesh net.
Taking of rare or threatened species.
Aquatic pollution.

There is no sufficient protection for "another fishing ground for the province," as labeled by the Samar Province LGU website. Of course, it's just another one of many.

It is heartening to see on government websites that there are funds from the national government that are funneled to the locals, but every time I ask Nanay and Tatay, there is always something missing with the should-be-constructed, should-be-finished items. Paper claims always exceed the facts. What's clear though is that the unliquidated cash advances amount to almost Php 19 million from 2001 to 2020.

This must be a different kind of panalipdanan, a very strong oracion that, even if it's already a new generation managing the town, old plans still seem nowhere in sight. In 2015, 68 years after the founding of Talalora as a town, there is still a 47.12% poverty incidence rate, nearly half of a population not even ten thousand strong. Perhaps it's also we who willfully perpetuate this kind of hurón.

WHEN I voted in 2019, I felt good. My duty was finished after shading the ballot and making sure that the voting receipt was exact. I even thought that the same family that has ruled the town since 2010 would finally be replaced.

I was still lining up for our polling precinct when I started to itch. There were just a few nips here and there, so I thought that they were only gnats because there were a lot of plants at the school. But I also started feeling unwell, so I went home immediately after voting. My rashes only appeared after I took half a bath. It was German measles. I had rashes all over my face, back, and thighs. I lay in bed that day and the ones after it for almost a week. Not only because I had swelling even up to my face, but also because my body felt weakened, not just the muscles but also the joints. I did not feel dizzy, but my lymph nodes became prominent, and I couldn't walk well because I couldn't seem to straighten my legs. I had to crawl if I wanted to sleep upstairs because of the fresh breeze.

We had two tambalans come to the house. The woman used an egg to divine my sickness. She would call the souls of our beloved dead one by one, and if the egg stood upright at the mention of one name, then I was said to be "gin-ungaraan" by that soul.

It was the male tambalan who succeeded. According to him, it was my great-grandparents who were responsible for my sickness. That's why we held a pangadi, a kind of prayer offering for the dead, after the male tambalan performed the takdom and rubbed lana, or coconut oil, on my limbs.

Sometimes, when a soul makes an ungara, it is appeased through a prayer offering. Sometimes they want to fuss over us, albeit in a non-physical form, like they did when they were still alive; sometimes they just want to be remembered. They could also be appeased through takdom or tayhop. The tambalan whispers an oracion or hudim-hudim to the head.

If you have had an ugmad or shock due to fear, sometimes luon is also applied. You are covered by a blanket while the tambalan chants, encircling you with a coconut shell with embers.

Basta, if the sickness is sudden and lasts for more than a day, we go to the tambalan immediately to make sure.

The powers of the tambalan and the barangan were also something of an inheritance before, and there were many rituals to be performed either in church or at the cemetery. In Nay Polen's stories, those who inherited these powers were often tall and well-built people. Our family was also noted for this in the olden days, but her father did not follow the required rituals anymore. My other uncle's knowledge is only limited to the takdom. Now, it is Nay Polen's daughter who has followed her footsteps, performing the pangadî.

It has changed since Japanese times. "After liberation, people changed; these things were controlled. Talalora became a municipality; people were able to go to school… There is no one performing these kinds of mischief anymore."

Perhaps Tatay also sees these beliefs of ours as some kind of tomfoolery; that's why he always keeps his distance whenever we opt for the bisayâ way of healing. He was a sanitary inspector after all and had already learned of the new ways. Had he believed in the diwatador, those who rigorously practiced superstitious beliefs, he might have said, "The diwatador have already died out, yet here you are still." Persisting in the belief of the gintatahas and turumanon, the obligations that needed to be fulfilled, and the sicknesses that only the hilot or massage could heal.

I was cured of my illness after a few days. I took paracetamol as medication, as Tatay told me. I also just had a hilot from a newcomer who married one of our townsmen. She passed the TESDA (Technical Education and Skills Development Authority) certification test. She told me that I had too many cold spots in my body, so I had to limit my exposure to the breeze. I had to close the windows because our breeze on shore is an aircon without an off switch.

I DON'T KNOW how we got there—my youngest sister, Ivy, and I—to Tiya Lucing's house. Ivy calls her "Mama" because Tiya Lucing was the one who took care of them when they were young and kept house while Nanay and Tatay were working. It was the summer of 2017, and I had just come home from a teaching stint in Cebu. Ivy had stopped college for a while and wanted to shift degrees. We had a lot to do that harvest season; we only lacked the will to do so. We agreed to walk around early in the morning.

"Let's go to Tulac, 'Ma!"

"Balitaw gad? You might not have been there yet; it's far."

"Sus, not a big deal. We'll go slowly."

Balitaw, we were strolling like it was a moonlit night. The morning breeze was bracing while it was the old people who were still awake. It was not sunny either, so our walk was very pleasant. We passed by a lot of rice fields where the carabaos lay in the muddy shade. We also went past Nay Polen's farmland, where there were a lot of santol (*Sandoricum koetjape*), which we used to buy often, especially when it was fiesta season, because they were big and sweet.

Mostly, I just listened to Tiya Lucing and Ivy. I was not that close to Tiya Lucing because I was already in school when she came to the house. Basta if Nanay and Tatay were on the dawn trip to Catbalogan, I accompany my younger sisters and we sleep at Tiya Lucing's house. Sometimes she calls me if she wants her uban plucked. I get one peso for twenty white hairs. If she calls my younger siblings, whom she was taking care of, they get two pesos. Tiya Lucing was not strict, but she also didn't spoil us with our whims.

On the second day of our morning walk, Ivy chose the Placer route to the south. We talked mostly about the future, especially because I also told Tiya Lucing that I was planning to go to Manila. But we weren't able to push through to Placer because the foot path was muddy, and Ivy and I wore rubber shoes. The road was also unlike the eastward road to Tulac, where the road was already flattened because it was supposedly going to be concretized, so the foot path was only fit for one person at a time and was a bit rocky. We went shoreward instead of to Kankastro.

Tiya Lucing was still with us when we went home because our house was closer to the shore than hers. Nanay was a little surprised that our hike lasted until eight in the morning, but she immediately asked Ivy to make coffee for Tiya Lucing. They mostly talked of when we were younger, when Tiya Lucing was still at home. It was easy banter, mainly because Tiya Lucing was also easy to talk with.

On the third day, Ivy didn't come with us anymore. Perhaps she was exhausted, so it was only Tiya Lucing and I who made the hike to the Tulac route. The electric wire almost sagging to the ground was still there, still unfixed, even if the barangay officials were reportedly alerted about it already.

We reached the boundary between Tulac and the población earlier than the previous days, so we continued hiking. We were following the trail of the road that was to be built, but it only reached Mallorga, the nearest barangay to Villareal. The road was still quite unsafe because it was narrow, rocky, and sometimes hiked upward, but some adventurous motorcycle riders could already pass through.

"Ano, shall we continue?" Tiya Lucing asked as we reached Mallorga. When it was low tide, the sea would ebb so far that it made it very easy to look for shellfish, but there was almost none now because of the quarrying.

"Sige gad, Tiya. I don't feel tired yet."

"Asya. Make the most of this because you don't really go outside your house."

We will go along the coast, said Tiya Lucing, so that we won't get lost. We finally reached Salagan, still part of Mallorga. From the hill spot where we took a rest, we could see the wide seas in between the islets. Some kids even stared at us when we passed by them in the barrios, abitapa, *these ones don't belong here.* When we came back to the border between Tulac and the población, the dew on the cassava stalks had already vaporized. Before, Tiya Lucing used to make puto out of cassava with coconut conserve in the middle. When the pandesal had run out before I reached rawis near the wharf or the street corner, I would go to their house to buy the cassava puto for breakfast. One whole cassava puto with two buns cost two pesos then. Tiya Lucing said that there were only a few who put up with cassava planting because the others were already on the 4Ps list.

I had thought that Tiya Lucing left us then because Ivy was already big and did not need tending to anymore. It turns out, as Nanay said, that Tiya Lucing hardly went back to our house when she joined the election campaign of the previous administration, which was practically just handed over to the present one. In the previous elections, while we thought that the winds would change, Tiya Lucing still stood by her choices.

We had gone back to only greeting each other on the street.

We didn't go back on the dirt road anymore after our almost ten-kilometer hike.

SOMETIMES, when I get too cross, I still hanker after a needle. Sometimes I also brag about this and tease others. But I always stop short because I don't carry a sewing kit, and I remember that we didn't even follow those traditions. The line was already severed before I was even born. Only the shadows of desires remain. I don't even know whether they really use needles or if I only get those from TV shows.

Nanay told me that coming from Talalora wasn't much of a hindrance to them when they were still studying. All the same, even if almost four generations have strayed from the turumanon, the blot persists.

There are a lot of beliefs that are only meant to scare people because nature is vengeful, particularly when it is violated, Nanay explains. But if the sea is already dirty and the hills are already bare, where do the dagatnon and the kahoynon dwell to take revenge?

We are changing the face of the hurón. The beliefs of old, which were only reserved for the powerful spirits, are now projected to the powerful officials of the town. *Don't touch. Don't say anything if you see something strange. Don't point fingers because if you do, your hand will rot.* Today, the list of those we are losing goes ever longer:

The fish which Nanay said used to come close even on their first dip at sea when they were younger.

The rattan vine named talolora which was used to name our town but was already bought only in Catbalogan during Nay Polen's time.

The mamban tree which Nanay hasn't even seen so it only lives as a saying when she tells us stories about our grandparents.

I wonder who will remember them when it is only in stories that they are heard.

I wonder who will remember those, who even in stories, are forgotten— those who are remembered only when the body groans in sickness.

How will we understand when to wound and when to heal?

2015 data reveals that Talalora's average population is getting younger: there are 72 youth dependents for every 100 working-age people, while there are only 11 elderly dependents. It is not a bad thing that most of our generation wields the pen already instead of the bolo, but often, through these means, we also distance ourselves from the moist earth. I don't yearn for the days when one's nose can be chipped with just a point of a finger. Buyag, may it be far from us. My mind only dwells on the stories that we haven't inherited—the wildernesses we have to go to other places for because our own is already bare. The old trees are uprooted and felled even before the new ones take root. Even Nay Polen has gone on to eternity.

LIFE is only changed, not ended.

Those who are lost become part of the kingdom of the unseen. They have released themselves from earthly signs.

Second lesson: *Remember, the world is in truth enchanted.*

An mga Taga-hurón

"TAGA-Talalora ka ngay-an? Diba damo it barangan ha iyo?"

Kadamo na gud hin nagpakiana hini ha ak nga waray na ak pakaihap.

Ngan an pirmi ko nga baton, "Oo. Han una." Di ngani, "Waray naman." O, "nagkamatay na."

Magkadirodilain la nga pulong para han usa nga karuyag sidngon: naglabay na.

Pero amo gud ito 't'am pangilal-an. Pangitaon mo ngani ha Internet, pirmi gud magsapit it "Talalora" ngan hit "barang." Karuyag sidngon, "haven of faith healers," siring pa han usa nga article han Philippine News Agency (PNA). Amo ini han una han nanunuod pa an kadam-an han mga kahoynon, mga dagatnon nga espiritu. Yana, natuod na la ada kon nadidisgrasya na.

SYAHAN nga pagturon-an hit pakig-ukoy ha kalibutan: *Ayaw paglabti it mga hayop, labi na adton gudti, kay diri ka man gin-aano.*

Syempre diri api hini an mga bangkâ, yatot, ulalahipan, ngan iba nga peste ha panimalay. Ini para la han mga taguto, bágang, imalay nga halas, ngan iba pa nga hayop nga bangin nawawara la hit ira dalan. Pinapabay-an la hira umoli, ngan kon sirado na it balay, gin-aabrihan an mga garawsan. Danay ha portahan, danay ha bintana, di ngani ha mga lu-ang han tabla nga salóg han am daan nga ruwang. Diri liwat ginpapalabtan it mga kamanampan ha pagtuo nga bangin it iba ha ira mga panalipdanan la.

Lakip an mga tanom ngan puno hini nga pagturon-an. Labot la han mga banwa, diri sadang gabuton an mga gatás-gatás, herba buena, ngan iba pa. Kon magpupulod man, ginsasaritan an puno upod an mga tambalan nga amo an nag-uuna han seremonyas, siring pa, amo an nagwi-whispering hope. Diri puydi nga bis ano la an ginkukuha.

Han bata pa kami, diri ngani kami pinapagmulay gud hadto han mga banwaon nga dapit, di ngani adton hagrani ha mga puno kay bangin mag-aringasa kami ngan makapukaw kami han mga diri-sugad-ha-at nga nangangaturog. Kon harayo pag-uli ha balay para han CR, kinahanglan manabi anay san-o umihi ha may puno. Angay gud magmatinahuron labi na hit mga puno kon nadiri nga darahugan.

Puydi liwat nga tawo mismo it makasakit, ngan dida hini nagtikang an pangilal-an han Talalora komo barangan. Siring pa ni Nay Polen, dadâ ni Nanay, "Bantog an Talalora han barang palakad, nakanhi ito dinhi ngatanan."

Nahitataraán ngani hit barang palakad, karuyag sidngon nakaági ka hin lugar nga gin-orasyonan hin usa nga tawo, asya nasasakit ka hin tigda o lain la nga klase hin disgrasya.

Puydi ka liwat mahiloan, labi na kon nakimas la hin kaon kon patron. Nakakapasakit gihap ini hin tubtob tulo ka adlaw, labi na kon ha karne humunob. Amo gihap ini nga nakadto ngani kami komo choir ha mga baro-barangay upod ni Padre kon nagmimisa hiya, nagdadara gud kami hin amon kalugaringon nga tubig irimnon.

Han kadaan nga tiyempo, duro gud kakusog an gahum han mga himangnoan. Siring pa ni Nay Polen, "… an mga tawo hadto siring ni Tatay, isakto la tudlukon" ngan puydi ka mapungag pareho kan Apoy Banô. Diri sugad hit mga nakikita ha TV nga kinahanglan pa hin buhok, di ngani monyika nga pagtutusukon hin dagom. Mayda ngani hadto oracion nga ginyayamyam parà diri ka makit-an, dako an bulig labi na han tiempo Hapon nga makuri an kabutang.

KON kikitaon ha mapa, lima la it mga island municipalities hit Samar: Tagapul-an, Almagro, Sto. Niño, Daram, ngan Zumarraga. Nahihimo na la nga isla kunohay it Talalora kay puro la pambot it gamit pagbiyahe tipa-Catbalogan o Tacloban. 2017 pa han mag-ikabiriling hin pondo an gobernadora para han 1.1 bilyon unta nga kalsada tikang ha Villareal ngadto ha am, para mas masarosayon pagbiyahe ngan diri na madelatar labi kon mabalud.

Kon kalsada ngan iba pa nga imprastraktura it paghihimangrawan, mayda na kwarta.

14.1 milyones nga kalsada tikang ha Poblacion Dos ngadto ha Tulac ha may tipa-Villareal nga ruta ha este, pero waray pa ginpagawas nga budget an Department of Budget and Management (DBM) dida han 2017.

4.4 milyones nga kalsada ha may tipa-Tacloban ha may timog, magdudugtong han barangay Placer ngan barangay Malaguining, an giharayoi nga baryo ngan usa nga geographically isolated and disadvantaged area (GIDA) ha Eastern Visayas, sumala han 2020 nga asoy han Department of Health (DOH). Tikang ha Placer, mas madali na la pagbiyahe ngadto ha Poblacion kay sementado naman kuno an agian nga ginsusubay han mga estudyante ngan iba pa nga nagbabaktas la kon mabalud. Amo ini an kaagi han akon dadâ nga nagbibinaktas hin sobra oras para la makauli tikang han iya pagminaestra, labi na kon maghumbas ha Placer kay subaón ini. Diri ngani puydi magdungan it duha nga motor pagsulod kay kipot hin duro it tikadto hit ira duruongan.

Balor 5.4 milyones nga pondo nga ginpagawas han DBM para han evacuation center namon ha Poblacion Dos. Ini kahuman mahiasoy dida han

2016 governance assessment report nga waray kami makapasar han ira kray-terya hin disaster preparedness ngan environmental management. Mayda na mga piktyur ha website han Department of the Interior and Local Government (DILG) nga pinanindugan na hin steel bars an napili nga lugar, pero sumala liwat han report han municipal accountant, waray pa tikangi pagtukod.

Amo ini an nahibaroan han 2018 nga Fisheries Compliance Audit:

Waray kami dyes porsyento nga area limit han aquaculture sugad han fish farming.
Waray kinse porsyento nga area para han fishery reserves.
Waray paglimitar han pangisda bisan pinaagi hin closed season.
Waray tinaglawas tikang han mga mangirisda.
Mayda gad mga fishery sanctuaries ngan limitasyon han gindadakop nga isda.
Pero mayda gihap diri awtorisado nga pangisda.
Panbadil.
Panguha ngan pamaligya hin bagangbang.
Pangisda gamit hin mga singpot.
Pandakop hin mga talagsaon nga hayop.
Polusyon ha dagat.

Waray igo nga proteksyon para han "usa han mga fishing ground han probinsya," siring pa han Samar Province LGU website. Syempre, usa gud la han damo pa kalain.

Makalilipay gad pagkikita ha mga website han gobyerno nga mayda pondo tikang han gobyerno nasyonal nga nahingangadto ha lokal, pero pagpapakiana ko kanda Nanay ngan Tatay, pirmi may kulang hit mga unta-gintitindog, unta-human na. Pirmi sobra it papel ha kamatuoran. Basta kay it klaro, harani disinuybe milyones it unliquidated cash advances tikang pa han 2001 ngada han 2020.

Lain gud ada ini nga klase nga panalipdanan, duro kakusog nga oracion nga bisan bag-o na nga henerasyon it nakapot hit pamunoan han bungto, diri la gihapon kinikita an mga daan pa nga plano. Bisan han 2015, saysenta y otso anyos kahuman mahimo nga bungto an Talalora, 47.12 porsyento la gihap an amon poverty incidence rate, harani katunga han bug-os nga populasyon nga diri ngani maabot hin napulo ka libo nga tawo. Bangin kami-kámi la gihap it tinuyo nga nagpapadayon hit sugad hini nga pagti-naga-hurón.

PAGBOTOS ko han 2019, maupay an ak pamati. Human na an ak obligasyon kahuman ko itomi an ak balota ngan siguradoha nga sakto an nakada han ak resibo. Kahuna ko pa mababalyoan na gihapon an amo la gihap nga pamilya nga nakapot han am bungto tikang pa han 2010.

Napila pa la ada ak hadto para han am presinto han magtinikang ako pagkatli. Gudti-gudti gad la nga katol sanglit kahuna ko nga bangin kanan tagnok la kay damo an mga tanom ha iskuylahan. Pero kay baga naglain na liwat an ak pamati asya nga umoli ako dayon kahuman ko bumotos.

Kahuman ko paglabar, asya pa la an panhataw han mga pula nga lapaka ha ak lawas, tipdas ha hangin. Lukop gud hasta ha nawong, likod, ngan mga páa. Hadto gud nga adlaw ngan han mga sumunod, haros usa ka semana, naghinigdaon la ako. Diri la tungod nga haros nanhupong liwat ako pati ha nawong, kundi tungod nga nagluya liwat an ak kalawasan, diri gud la an kauondan kundi haros pati an mga tul-an. Diri malipong an ak ulo pero ginlisayan ako ngan waray ak pakakalakat hin tadong kay diri ak nakakaunat hin maupay han akon mga tiil. Ginkakamang ko nala an mga balitang han am hagdanan kon ha igbaw ako nakaturog para puropresko it hangin.

Duha an am ginpakadto nga tambalan ha balay. An pamaagi han babaye hin pagtigó amo in pinatindog nga bonay. Gintatawag niya tag-usa-usa an mga kalag han am mga nawára ngan kon tumindog an bonay pagtawag han ngaran, amo an nag-ungara ha ak.

An lalaki nga tambalan an nakatigo. Nasiring hiya, gin-ungaraan ako han akon mga kaapoy-apoyan, asya nga nagpapangadi kami kahuman ako niya takdomi ngan banyosan hin lana ha butkon.

Danay it mga kalag nga naungara, gintutumanan la hin pag-ampo kay napahinumdom. Danay liwat naugay la, bisan diri na ha pisikal nga pamaagi, sugad han binubuhat nira han buhi pa hira. Puydi liwat madara hin takdom o tayhop. Ginhuhudim-hudiman hit tambalan it mubon-búbon.

Kon ugmad dara hit kahadlok, danay ginluluonan pa. Ginlulukop ka hin taklap ngan ginpapaasohan hin bága dida hit bagol samtang nagyayamyam it tambalan nga nalibot ha imo.

Basta kon tigdaay la nasakit ngan nasobra na hin usa ka adlaw, napatambalan dayon kami pagkasigurado.

Surundanon gihap an gahum han mga tambalan ngan barangan hadto ngan mayda ini mga turumanon, di ngani ha singbahan, ha kamposanto. Siring pa ni Nay Polen, an mga namamagsunod hini kaurogan dagko nga mga tawo, mga hagtaas. Bantugan ngani an am pamilya hadto, pero kay waryó na magsunod an iya tatay. An akon usa nga tiyo, tubtob takdom na la an maaram. Yana, an anak na ni Nay Polen an nagsunod ha iya komo paropangádi.

Nagbag-o na tikang han tiyempo Hapon. "Han pag-liberation na kay baga nagkakokontrol naman, iba naman an mga tawo. Nagin munisipyo na, nag-papakaiskuyla na man… Waray naman baga namamaglinuog-luog yana."

Linuog-luog gud la liwat ada it kita ni Tatay hito nga am mga tuluohan asya napahirayo hiya hin napabisayâ kami hin tambal. Sanitaryo man gud hiya, nakag-aram na han mga kinabag-ohan nga kinaadman. Kon natuod pa hiya han mga diwatador, masiring gud ada nga, "Nagkamatay na la an mga diwatador, adi ka pa nasasalin." Napabilin pagtuo han mga gintatahas ngan mga turumanon, han mga sakit nga hilot la it nakakaupay.

Naupay man gihap ako han ak sakit paghagos han pira ka adlaw. Ginpatumar la ako ni Tatay hin paracetamol. Nagpahilot la liwat ako han usa nga dayo nga nakaasawa hin taga-amon. Nakapasar hiya ha TESDA (Technical Education and Skills Development Authority). Nasiring hiya damo kuno an ak taghom ha lawas asya waray la anay ako magpinahangin hin ura-ura. Kinahanglan panadhan an mga bintana kay it am hangin ha baybay amo in erkon nga waray parung-parong.

AMBOT ANO man adto nga nahingadto kami han ak manghod nga hi Ivy kanda Tiya Lucing. "Mama" an tawag ni Ivy kay hi Tiya Lucing an nagbabantay ha ira han guti pa hira ngan naglilimpyo ha balay samtang nagtratrabaho hira Nanay ngan Tatay. Summer adto han 2017 ngan pag-uuli ko pa la tikang han ak pagtutdo ha Cebu; hi Ivy humunong anay pag-iskuyla kay karuyag mag-shift. Damo an buruhaton hadto nga katbarî, pagbuot na la an kulang. Nagkasarabot kami pag-walking.
"Tulac kita, 'Ma!"
"Balitaw gad? Bangin waray ka pa hingadto, harayo baya."
"Sus, diri gad ito. Hinay-hinay gad la kita."
Baga la balitaw kami hin namamasyada hin bulanon. Nakakapukaw an hangin han aga-aga samtang haros mga kalagsan pa la an nagmamata. Diri liwat adto masirak sanglit maupay la paglinakat. Damo an mga hagna nga am naagian, diin nanlulunay an mga kakarabwan ha may lagyon nga lindong. Nakaagi pa kami han may uma nira Nay Polen diin damo an santol nga amo an amon súkot paliton han una labi kon patron kay dagko ngan magtam-is.
Haros nagpipinamati la liwat ako han istorya nira tungod nga diri man gud ako súok kan Tiya Lucing kay naiskuyla naman ako han mahingadto hiya ha balay. Basta kon nasakay hira Nanay hin maagahon tipa-Catbalogan, gin-uupdan ko la liwat hira Ivy ngan didto kami nakaturog kanda Tiya Lucing. Kon napakuha hiya hin uban, danay ako an gintatawag. May piso ako kon nakakakuha ak hin baynte nga uban. Kon an ak mga manghod nga iya binantayan an iya ginsusugo, dos an hatag. Diri hiya istrikto, pero diri man liwat duro an pagpatungyo han am mga kinakaruyag.
Han ikaduha ka adlaw han am pagbinaktas, tipa-Placer naman ha may timog an ginpili nga ruta ni Ivy. Puro tiarabot an am istorya hadto labi kay ginsumat ko liwat nga tipa-Manila unta ako. Pero waray kami kadayon ha may Placer kay lapukon pa an dalan ngan nagpaka-rubber shoes kami ni Ivy. Diri liwat sugad han dalan pa-este ngadto ha Tulac nga pinatag na kay hihimuon kuno nga kalsada, asya kanan pan-usa ka tawo la it agian ngan batuon pa. Nagtipabaybay lugod kami ha may Kankastro.
Upod pa nam hi Tiya Lucing pag-uli kay haroharani an am balay ha baybay. Napausa hi Nanay nga na-alas otsohan an am pagbinaktas pero ginpatimplahan dayon kan Ivy hin kape hi Tiya Lucing. Sige an ira istorya han ira kaagi, han nakadto pa hi Tiya Lucing ha balay. Madali-dali la an mga sunlog labi na nga lingaw liwat hiya nga kaistorya.

Han ikatulo ka adlaw, waray na umupod hi Ivy. Gin-gul-an ada asya kami na la nga duha ni Tiya Lucing an nagbaktas ha may Tulac nga ruta. Nakadto la gihap an kawad han kuryente nga haros kumanay na ha tuna, waray pa katadong bisan ginreport na kuno ha barangay.

Tirutimprano kami nga nahiabot ha utlanan han Tulac ngan han población asya nagpadayon la gihap kami. Baga ginsusubay liwat namon an dalan nga hihimuon nga kalsada pero tubtob la ini ha Mallorga, an gihar-aani nga baryo ha Villareal. Baga delikado pa ngani an dalan kay kipot, batuon, ngan usahay tipahataas ha bukid, pero nakakaagi na an mga dudya-ganon magminotor.

"Ano mapadayon pa kita?" pakiana ni Tiya Lucing paghingadto namon ha may Mallorga. Halapad an hurubasan hini diin han hadto damo an pangti-on, pero haros waray na yana kay gin-quarry na man.

"Sige gad, Tiya. Diri pa man mapaol."

"Asya. Singabot gud kay diri ka naggagawas-gawas ha iyo."

Subay la kuno kami ha baybay, siring ni Tiya Lucing, para diri kami mawara. Hasta nga nahiabot kami ha may Salagan, sakop pa han Mallorga. Tikang ha amon ginhunongan nga dapit ha bukid, tan-aw an haluag nga dagat butnga han mga isla. Ginkikinitaan pa kami han kabataan nga am naaagian ha mga baryo, abitapa, *diri man ini taga-dinhi.* Paghibalik nam ha may utlanan ha Tulac ngan han bungto, singaw na an anay tun-og ha mga dawhog han bilanghoy. Hadto, ginpuputo ni Tiya Lucing an bilanghoy ngan ginbubutangan hin konserba nga lubi ha butnga. Kon waray na ako nahiaabtan nga pandesal ha rawis, di ngani ha eskina, nakadto ako ha ira pagpapalit hin pamahawon. Tag-dos adto hadto an magtakop. Guti na la kuno it nag-aagwanta pagbilanghoy kay damo na man it naka-4Ps.[1]

Kahuna ko umiwas hi Tiya Lucing ha balay han una tungod nga dagko na hira Ivy ngan diri na barantayan. Ngayan, nasiring hi Nanay, haros waray na pakakabalik hi Tiya Lucing ha balay han mag-inupod hiya han kampanya ha eleksyon han dati nga administrasyon nga haros iginpasa la han yana. Ngan han una nga eleksyon, samtang kahuna namon nga mababag-o na an huyob han hangin, amo la gihap an tindog ni Tiya Lucing.

Bumalik na liwat kami han asihay la kon nagkakatapo.

Waray na kami pakag-walking utro kahuman hadto nga am haros dyes kilometros nga baktas.

DANAY gad, kon duro tak kauriton, naikakuruha la gihap ako hin dagom. Danay ngani ginpapanhambog ko pa ngan gintitiaw ha iba. Pero pirmi gud diri nahinanayon kay waray man ak dara-dara nga tarahian, ngan nahinu-numdoman ko nga waray man kami liwat mamagmamat hito nga mga surundanon. Waray pa ako ig-anak, maiha na nga nautod an linya. Lambong na la hin mga ungara it nahibibilin. Diri ngani ako maaram kon dagom gud ba it ira gingagamit, o kun mga salida na la ha TV it nagsusumat hito.

Nasiring hi Nanay, waray man makaulang an ira pagkataga-Talalora han nangingiskuyla hira. Pero amo gud ito, bisan kon haros upat na ka henerasyon an waray magsunod han mga turumanon, naulat gud it una nga tatak.

Damo nga mga tuluohan it panhadlok la tungod nga dumtanon it kalibongan labi na kon gintatalapas ini, esplikar ni Nanay. Pero kay kon mahugaw na it dagat, kon hawan na it kabukiran, hain pa man nahúron an mga dagatnon ngan kahoynon nga manhihimalos?

Ginbabag-o ta it dagway hit hurón. An mga tuluohan hiunong han anay mga gamhanan nababalhin na ha mga gamhanan han bungto. *Ayaw paglabot. Ayaw hin mugo kon nakita hin mga urusahon. Ayaw panudlok kay madudunot tim kamot.* Yana, natikahalaba an taramdan han mga naaanaw:

An kaisdaan nga siring nira Nanay nadaop dayon pagtunlob pa la nira ha dagat han bata pa hira.

An talolora nga oway nga amo an iginngaran ha am bungto pero panahon pa la nira Nay Polen ha Catbalogan na la ginpapalit.

An puno han mamban nga bisan hi Nanay waray pa makakita asya nabubuhi na la ha pananglitan hin nag-iistorya hiya han am mga kaapoy-apoyan.

Hino daw an manhihinumdom hini ha ira kon ha istorya na la nababatian.

Hino daw an manhihinumdom hadton bisan pati ha istorya, nahingalimtan. Napasakit na la para mahinumdoman.

Aanhon ta pagsabot kon sano magtatambal, ngan sano magsasamad?

Naasoy an 2015 nga datos nga natikabata it populasyon hit Talalora: mayda sitenta y dos nga mga kabataan nga nadepender ha kada usa ka gatos ka tawo nga nananarabaho, samtang onse la an mga kalagsan. Diri gad maraot nga bolpen na, diri bolo, it kinaptan hit kadam-an, kundi kaurogan tungod hini nga pamaagi, nahaharayo gihap kita hit humog nga tuna. Diri ako naungara han mga adlaw nga isakto la tudlukon, napupungag dayon. Buyag, ipahirayo. Nahúron la tak hunahuna hadton mga istorya nga waray na namon kahimamat, han mga hurón nga gindadayo pa kay haros hawan naman ha amon. Nagkakagagabót, nagkakapupulód it mga daan nga puno samtang diri pa nakakag-ugat an mga bag-o. Bisan hi Nay Polen, nag-una na ha kadayonan.

IT kinabuhi diri napapas, igo la nga nababalhin.[2]

Nababalhin na an mga naanaw ha ginhadian han mga diri kinikita. Nakabuhi na hira han mga tunan-on nga panigamnan.

Ikaduha nga pagturon-an: *Hinumdomi, it kalibutan balitaw tawoan.*

NOTES
1. Pantawid Pamilyang Pilipino Program.
2. Line from the Mass Preface for Christian Death.

Borneo Reborn

We are climate refugees here in the New World. Although five generations of colonists have eked out more than mere existence here, far from our motherland, Planet Earth, we still view ourselves as novices.

With all their scientific and technological know-how, the first colonists tried to recreate life on Earth. We are still trying. It is our motherland after all, the unique place of beauty and bounty that gave birth to life—to the animals and the plants, to the *Homo sapiens* we are—so it is natural that we should try to recreate it on the new planet. This time, without mistakes. This time, for eternity. The dream, nay, the aim is to allow life to carry on in perpetuity. This is perhaps what the ancients would say courts hubris, while the original born-again believers say this is a doomed, corrupt world and they can live forever only in the next world. We colonists believe it is possible for us to recreate life as it was meant to be on Planet Earth, as it was in the fabled Garden of Eden, so that there is a new planet Earth that is pristine and self-sustaining, untouched by malice, greed, and selfishness.

In this new, recreated, replicated world, we can give birth to new members of our species and sustain not just our own lives but also the flora and fauna that once thrived on Planet Earth. That is, we are trying to do this. It is a tremendous responsibility to bear, and we colonists are aware of this. Every new birth on the planet is a joyous occasion, but it is also a serious event. What will this child grow up to contribute in the future? What talents and skills will this infant possess? Will she become a productive member of society, or will he become a delinquent who needs to be exiled back to our dying motherland?

The society I work in and live in is the one that my ancestors were born into, of course. We are recreating Borneo, the Borneo that had once been one of Planet Earth's most diverse biological hotspots. Our ancestors lived to see the extinction of the Sumatran rhino in our country, Malaysia, all the way back in 2019. When my life and work on this colony planet seem fruitless or impossible, I think of the story of that solitary captured female, Iman, dying alone, guarded at Sabah's Tabin Wildlife Reserve, treated over the lonely years but failing to reproduce by the country's final elderly male rhino, Tam. She finally succumbed to cancer. This followed the death of the other captured female, Puntung, who had to be euthanized. Such was her suffering. Their stories haunt me, but they also spur me on. We are witnessing our own species' cruel demise on a dying planet. The planet we destroyed—sending greenhouse gases into the atmosphere, causing the melting of icebergs, snowy peaks, and glaciers, flooding and warming the oceans, the sea levels rising and drowning whole islands, and making homeless nations of people.

We are trying to bring life back to this new Borneo, a better Borneo, with a population of more knowledgeable, more caring, more selfless, and more kind people. We will not take this New World for granted. And we will not be selfish and greedy. Which is why the delinquents are exiled to the dying Earth, which was ravaged and destroyed by our ancestors. We cannot allow the same mistakes to be repeated in this newly created paradise.

Each country has been given a share of the new planet. We are to replicate our ancestors' cultures, languages, arts, and unique ways of life. That is, unique ways of life that do not drain the natural environment of their own lives. Yes, it sounds like an oxymoron, recreating a natural environment. Yet this really is our job. It is our purpose on this new planet, our second chance, one we never thought would actually be possible. So, for five generations now, we have tried and are still trying to recreate that natural environment, and when we finally do, we will make sure that it is sustainable. And we will learn from our past mistakes and treat them with respect.

I am on the team recreating the Semenggoh Wildlife Centre. It includes the nature reserve where semi-wild orang-utans lived and controversially procreated. Some argued that these semi-wild orang-utans were genetically dead, that they could never live in the wild again, and so should not be allowed to procreate. Others argued they would keep the species alive, and they must be encouraged to breed to stave off extinction. These were the confiscated animals, rescued from illegal wildlife traders or from local villagers who had captured infant orang-utans and reared the cute babies with tufts of red hair and huge round eyes as pets until they grew too large and too strong to be controlled.

Traumatized by the brutal killing of their mothers, raised by humans in cages or in human homes, sometimes dressed in human clothes, these confiscated animals were then taught by the keepers at the nature reserve how to climb trees, make their own nests, and forage for food in the pockets of rainforests surrounded by villages. If deemed sufficiently rehabilitated, they were left alone to be semi-wild, living in the nature reserve, emerging once or twice a day only when they could not find fruits and figs or when they heard the call of their human cousins. Then, they would come to the feeding platforms to enjoy bananas, papayas, and even durians in front of gawking crowds of visitors. The records show that up to 30,000 tourists would visit Semenggoh Wildlife Centre in a single month before the coronavirus pandemic reached even the remotest Bornean shores in that period of the plague, from early 2020 well into 2022.

What is it about the red ape that draws its *Homo sapiens* cousins? We have photographs and videos of semi-wild red apes who moved slowly and deliberately through the trees, approaching the feeding platforms where the keeper would be calling. We have books about the "man from the forest"—coffee table and academic books, collections of Iban stories about human and orang-utan relationships—human beings reincarnated as orang-utans, human maidens kidnapped by orang-utans and giving birth to strapping children who appeared like humans or orang-utans depending on what the situation called for.

There is also the mummified Bullet on a glass display at Matang Wildlife Centre to remind us of the most human of the orang-utans, shot in the head by the poachers who killed his mother. We are told that for every trafficked infant orang-utan, four or five adults and youngsters are killed or die on the road to the human world. They were endangered and faced extinction, but science has prevailed. We have brought them back to life here in the new Borneo. At least, they are the best that science can produce.

This morning, I woke up to another new day in Borneo Reborn, and I am thankful to see clear skies. The monsoon rains may come later in the day if the meteorologists have been able to do their work, but at least this morning, I will start the day dry. I walk up the winding road from the barracks to the wildlife center. It replicates the original wildlife center but is five times the size. We did not replicate the villages and fruit farms that surrounded the original wildlife center and nature reserve. We are trying to minimize the human-animal conflict. The semi-wild orang-utans should have enough forest and space to meander and forage without wandering into a farmer's orchard and getting shot for eating his fruit. I hope we have learned from our ancestors' mistakes.

I like to be the first one at the center every day. The morning is cool, and there is nothing but the sound of the birds chirping and the rustle of leaves in the trees. Somewhere in the dense foliage, the semi-wild orang-utans are foraging or maybe just resting in their nests. I wonder what they are thinking. Maybe they are thinking about searching for figs, or they are waiting for the call to the feeding platforms. Maybe they are wondering if they should move to the farthest corners of the nature reserve and make their way out to roam in the new world beyond those boundaries. They will find that the nature reserve is a huge bubble, and there is no way for them to break through that bubble, for outside is an uninhabitable world for any living creature, human or nonhuman.

The colonists sometimes ask why we need to replicate the wildlife center and the nature reserve and why we couldn't just let the orang-utans roam in the natural habitats they had been stolen from and which are being reborn into here in the New World. Wouldn't that have been the right thing to do? But the wildlife biologists couldn't be sure that the species they had recreated in a laboratory from the DNA of a semi-wild orang-utan would have the survival skills necessary for them to function in the wild. All indicators suggested that even the basic skills of climbing trees were learned behaviors. We know this from the orphaned orang-utans who had been captured for the wildlife pet trade and raised by humans instead of their biological mothers. All this misery started when Western explorers "discovered" the world and peaked during the miserable years of globalization, which our ancestors misguidedly believed was an indicator of human ingenuity and progress.

The DNA of wild orang-utans will be used to give birth to the *Pongo pygmaeus* released in the recreated Lanjak Entimau Wildlife Sanctuary (182,985 hectares) alongside the Batang Ai National Park (24,040 hectares) and Betung Kerihun National Park in what was formerly West Kalimantan (800,000 hectares). As in the original Planet Earth, combined, these formed the second largest protected area in Borneo, after the Kayan-Mentarang National Park (1,360,500 hectares) in East Kalimantan. The scientists hope the wild orang-utans will survive in the rebirthed, rich biodiversity hotspot. This large area of virgin tropical rainforest, with its labyrinth of waterways, is taking a long time to rebirth, and meanwhile, we must do the best we can with the semi-wild orang-utans in the nature reserve.

I know I am lucky to be a park ranger working here in Borneo Reborn. Every day, I walk in a tropical rainforest. Some of the colonists cannot bear the humidity and prefer the four seasons of the temperate zones. But there are rumors that those zones are not faring so well; it is not easy to vary the climate within a bubble every few months. Here in Borneo Reborn, my predecessors had even recreated the walkway to the old cages that once housed the adult orang-utans who had begun to exhibit aggressive behavior. This is to remind us of the damage inflicted on the infant red apes and the traumas they experience as they grow up in the nature reserve, with human caregivers that they imprint on. I wonder how the orang-utans process this cruel fate: living freely, learning to climb and roam in the foliage, seeking food, trying to make nests for themselves, and then, once they grow too large, strong, and aggressive, they are caged on the ground for the rest of their adult lives, which could be up to thirty years or so.

In our files, I find the write-up of a researcher who spoke to Abang Haji Kassim Abang Morshidi, a civil servant who worked his way up in the National Parks and Wildlife Office and who then became director of the Sarawak Tourism Board back in the 1970s. The paper tells us about the establishment of the Semenggoh Orang-utan Rehabilitation Centre and the poignant story of a young Bullet.

Instrumental in preventing the land from being taken over by the army to be used as a camp, Abang Haji Kassim Abang Morshidi helped to develop Semenggoh into a haven for confiscated endangered wildlife. These included gibbons and hornbills, as well as orang-utans. He and his wife, Madam Bibiana Pek, brought their children to the Semenggoh Orang-utan Rehabilitation Center one day. The young Bullet, the most famous of the confiscated orang-utans in Sarawak, reached out to the human mother and stroked her leg. He hugged her leg. Playful and happy, the young Bullet grew unrecognizable. Madam Bibiana told the researcher of her anger with the rangers who laughed at Bullet, thinking that he was a big joke and trying to be as human as they were. It is a sad, pitiful story.

I walk into Cage 14, where Bullet lived his final days. The trees loom over the cage. How they must have tempted him, but there was nothing for him to climb up to reach the branches and leaves. Even if there were, he would not have been able to climb through the cage.

I like to stand in the cage, close my eyes, and breathe in the smell of the rich earth and the humid air. I open my eyes slowly and fold my arms across my chest. This was Bullet's favorite stance. He is depicted this way in his mummified remains stored at the reborn Matang Wildlife Centre. I pace the cage as Bullet did. I imagine the visitors who came to peer at him— at the Australian and Japanese veterinarians who studied and cared for him.

Today, my colleague Tisen finds me in Cage 14.

"Analisa, what are you doing in there?" He is holding the tracker, checking on the locations of the semi-wild orang-utans.

"Nothing," I step out of the cage.

"Aren't you on feeding duty this morning?"

"Yes. I'm heading there now. I'll get the fruit and set up on the feeding platform now." I leave Tisen, mouth agape with another question not quite formed, and walk carefully on the planks, past the other cages where the gibbons and orang-utans once lived.

I wish that I could have been here when the infant Bullet lived his life again. I wish that I could have spoken to Madam Bibiana and told her that no one laughed at Bullet, that he had lived a full life, thirty-five years, with no rangers laughing at him and no veterinarian overdosing him with anesthetic.

I take out the fruit and lay them on the feeding platform: papayas, bananas, and jackfruit today. Cupping my hands over my mouth, I make the call of the orang-utan. The call echoes in the bubble. I call again. Then, I see the branches swaying and the leaves fluttering. It is the grand dame of the Semenggoh orang-utans: Seduku. She is the third-generation Seduku. The first and second did not last long in the rebirthed Semenggoh Nature Reserve. This third-generation Seduku (the first and original Seduku is not counted as the first generation; she is the original) has come further than her predecessors. She has been recorded mating with a third-generation Ritchie, but so far, she has not managed a live birth.

Ah. I see Ritchie moving slowly through the canopy. When he reaches the platform, Seduku has left with her bunch of bananas. She is not feeling social. This is unfortunate. I am watching her disappear when I feel Ritchie's hand grasp my wrist. He pulls me right up next to him, and before I can find my voice, he has clasped me by my waist against his body and is climbing up the ropes we strung up for the orang-utans to make their way to the feeding platform.

I believe in our mission, to recreate Planet Earth's best biodiverse hot-spots and to recreate the wildlife species that once roamed the real Earth. I believe that we must recreate the rebirthed Earth as closely as we can, and that the wildlife we rebirth must also be allowed to live as they did in their past lives. I have studied the legends as well as the biological tomes. I know well the legends that tell the stories of the old grandfathers who die and are born again as orang-utans, the stories of maidens snatched away by male orang-utans, and young men charmed to live in the treetops with the female orang-utans. In the shared lands of Batang Ai and Lanjak Entimau, these stories saved the orang-utans from the Iban people, who were famed for their hunting skills. The Iban believed the orang-utan were family and that they were descendants of the orang-utan-human line.

I remember these stories as Ritchie takes me up into the treetops. I realize that we have done what we set out to do. We have replicated the world that was once created on Planet Earth. This is the original world—the world we thought was that of legends. But that world is not a myth. These are true stories once lived by the early orang-utans and the early people in Borneo. Tisen will track me now as well as Ritchie, for I have a tracker implanted in my arm as all colonists do to keep us safe.

And it is true that I am safe. I will let the park rangers know this so they do not try to tranquilize Ritchie to tear me away. I will let them know they must let nature run its course. I am part of the study now for I won't try to escape. Even if I try, I don't believe Ritchie will let me go, unless Seduku can tempt him away. But I don't think she is interested.

Surely this is the greatest success a colonist in Borneo Reborn could have. To become a part of the beginnings of the human-orang-utan line. To be a part of the legend reborn.

KEVIN YANG

Notes on Plants

1.

For the past few summers
I've been trying my best
to grow vegetables,
a practice
I've always envied of my mother.

One year
it was eggplants
wanting nothing more than to hold
the fleshy fruit in my palms
only to watch the seedlings crushed
underneath hail in April.
Another year, it was beets
the joy of plucking each pink nugget
from the brown earth
only to realize that
I have no idea
how to eat a beet.
So I watch them wrinkle on the kitchen counter
happy enough to remember
they once started out
as seeds.

2.

When my parents first moved into their home
they spent weeks
unraveling rolls of sod hoping
to make their backyard fit into
the quiet suburban neighborhood
around them,
except,
for a massive patch of dirt

that sat right in the center of it.
From it, my parents
planted a garden.
Full of cucumbers,
full of chili peppers,
full of life.
Ask my parents what their favorite part of the house is
and they will most likely point you towards the garden.

3.

I've been learning about secondary forests
a phenomenon in which a new canopy of trees
grows out from the decay of the old growth forest
beneath it because of drought or disease or disaster.
The easiest way to find them is the clear break in the tree line,
a tall row of maples only to be punctuated by
a line of white birches beneath that seem out of place.
I can't help but see the different trees in my family,
Minnesota and Laos,
the break in the canopy like birch and maple,
somewhere between peace and war,
between gunshots on the Mekong River
and a warm bed in Minneapolis.
How does nature
transition so softly
from old growth to soft pine?

4.

There is an old Hmong folktale
where after surviving a flood
that destroys the rest of the world
brother and sister gave birth to their first child,
a grotesque being
resembling pumpkin more than human.
In their shock, they chop up their creation
and spread its remains across the earth.
Where each piece landed, another Hmong village was born.
Sometimes,
I stare at maps and remember this folktale,
run my finger across the countries,
and ask myself
what being sacrificed itself,
to allow us to be reborn again after this flood we called war,
our people scattered into the wind like seeds

catching root in every corner of the earth,
yet recognizing our common point of origin.
One time while traveling in Thailand,
I meet a Hmong kid,
born on the other side of the ocean
who tells me,
he too loves eating hot dogs and rice for breakfast
and it is in this moment
that I cannot help but believe
that we were all
cut from the same pumpkin.

5.
This year,
I've been trying to grow snow peas
watching each cup shoot a stem up towards the sky
too heavy for its own body.
Somehow,
each tendril reaches out towards the other
creating a canopy where they can all stand.
Four stems sprouting out from four different cups
no words exchanged
no special scaffolding needed
all aware
of how to keep
each other standing
of how
to keep each other
growing.

ERIC ABALAJON

*Letter to America: I [erasure]*_____

NOTES

Carlos Bulosan, known primarily for his autobiographical novel *America Is in the Heart* (1946), actually came out first with slim volumes of poetry a few years earlier, at the start of World War II. One of these volumes is *Letters from America* (1942), containing two poems with the same title as the collection, and this is an erasure of the first poem. They detail the environmental transformation of the Philippines under American colonial rule and the country's entry into the war; at the same time, Bulosan parallels these with passages of disenchantment as a migrant worker in the United States.

While an attempt to build links among oppressed classes in the metropole and the periphery, Bulosan's romanticism could easily be mistaken for ambivalence. This erasure project aims to make visible and imbue with renewed urgency the concerns Bulosan was preoccupied with decades ago. Ultimately, environmental deterioration is still closely linked to militarism and class stratification, and a way out of this planetary crisis is through solidarity among peoples.

"Letter to America: I" is accessed from Carlos Bulosan. *Letters from America*. Prairie City, IL: J.A. Decker, 1942.

LET   ME

       write
               the trees   leveled   to the ground
      fire   laughed and screamed,
                  the festival,   silenced
                            the history
Of leaves   shake
          the mountains   , the hills
              the rivers, and
                 the fields
                     the garden
             for the queen of spring
Is now   sleeping

I sit here   thinking of
Cities   like rain
But
                     pictures
      makes us
        scream for life,   men are
           burning   mountains   of sand,
Glass, paper   death is calling
For   trees

     we are
                 bleeding
           you.

JACQUELINE SHEA

Mother Divine

To my stepmom, Divina, and to Mama Earth.

She speaks of the Mountains
    of sending souvenirs of the American Dream across three seas,
        two lands,
      landing at the bottom of one hill.
    Her nephew rides his motorcycle down the dirt path,
      weaving through the greenery
        to retrieve it.
She reminisces over climbing trees and cracking coconuts
    at their ripest and drinking their fresh milk
      Supple in their mother-age
        unlike those stolen in their infancy
          unable to be cracked
        still protected by their youth.
She teaches me to make ube pie,
    mashing purple sweet potatoes from the Asian Market
      How they're not quite the same,
        the texture misses the target.
She honors the doctor quack-quacks
    Praising those living in the remote crevices
      using their healing hands
        providing vital medicine
        protecting against the nemesis
    Anointed by the Holy Book.
She speaks in Bisaya
    vis-à-vis Tagalog and English
    as she picks up wandering words in Spanish

denouncing her syncretistic sound
As her multilingual tongue
Dances across countless cultures,
and identities,
dog-whisperer
climber of trees
prayer of pleas
Lover of me.
A multifaceted being from land to sea,
igniting possibilities,
from island to island in fierce perseverance
my mother much more than her appearance
Weaving her way with or without clearance
A blend of essences
resilient,
present.

A tapestry of perspectives and lessons.

PHƯƠNG ANH

a dislocation

Yesterday-forward

    in tomorrow.

Unearthing

    to choreograph the seasons.

Autumn comes

    find home.

Winter ends

    the number has ripened.

Cross-pollination

    the nation.

But a birth-soil[1]

    outside the eye.

A footprint

    the areca tree.

I plant an incense[2]

    the homeless.

And I wander

    in search of you.

rain falls

warm bones

before the roots

only when

to salvage

only blooms

lay under

to shelter

in voiceless forest

NOTES
1. Nguyễn Thanh Hiện. *Chronicles of a Village.* Translated by Nguyễn Quyên-Hoàng, Penguin, 2022.
2. For more on the practice of incense in postwar ghost rituals, see Kwon Heonik. *Ghosts of War in Vietnam.* Cambridge University Press, Cambridge, 2008.

CHRISTIAN JIL R. BENITEZ

*Of Plants and Ghosts*_____

> *Even the wisest among you is only a conflict and mix of plant and ghost.*
> —Nietzsche

An SM mall stands less than a kilometer away from my house, right where my old school used to be. It blatantly calls itself an SM City Mall despite the fact that San Mateo, in the province of Rizal, is yet to become a city. Under the official jurisdiction, San Mateo is still classified as a first-class municipality, which means it is a town whose annual average income is only worth at least fifty-five million pesos, or roughly half of what a proper city is expected to earn. Unsurprisingly, there have been efforts to convert the town to a city, which have led to, among others, the annexation of San Mateo as a separate district of Rizal. To this day, however, the name of the mall ultimately remains an anachronism: it is a designation that still anticipates what is yet to come for my hometown. After all, cityhood seems to be the likeliest future for San Mateo, with its practical continuity with the adjacent cities of Quezon, Marikina, and Antipolo, which inevitably affect our town in terms of population, traffic, and perhaps even sensibility. As such, the large blue letters that spell the word CITY above the name SAN MATEO on the façade of the mall only literalize the looming further transformation of our town, as if after all this time, the building itself has not been enough of a reminder for the rapid developments that are happening in this place.

But the mall, it has to be said, does not merely predict or neutrally proclaim this future for San Mateo; instead, it also consciously persists to make sure that the cityhood it prematurely channels and marks ultimately becomes a reality, and moreso an inevitable one. For starters, it is also through this very shopping mall that San Mateo has generated more income since the mall's establishment more than seven years ago. At the time of its opening, with its strategic location near the three aforementioned cities as well as the neighboring municipality of Rodriguez, the mall was already estimated to serve a population of more than half a million people. And so, contrary to the celebratory statement of the president then of SM Supermalls on the opening of this particular branch, the company's mall expansions do not simply "focus… on these new growth cities where incomes and aspirations are showing significant improvement," but instead facilitate as well the perpetuation of what it considers progress. And for the movement toward this so-called growth, the mall becomes vital machinery for places such as San Mateo; it is what lures more people in, which is crucial for the endeavor to churn out more auditable income for the municipality as a whole. In this sense, the mall is what the colorful petals of a flower are to a bee.

"The color palette of the mall," as described by a press release from the company, "gets its inspiration from nature with the shaded array of green hues with a pixelated design." This "inspiration," however, does not necessarily mean—or could not possibly mean, at least not anymore—the mall being influenced by the immediate greenery of its surroundings, with the latter being hardly green now in the first place. A couple of years prior to the construction of the establishment, the large narra trees that once lined and canopied the main road of the town—trees that have witnessed the time when either sides of the same road were said to be open fields and San Mateo was yet to be paved into the concrete suburb it is now—were taken down and felled one by one, starting from the edge of the town bordering Marikina and toward the heart of the town, in order to make way for a wider main road. Said to help decongest the worsening traffic in our town, the project was thought to be necessary since this particular road connects the entire municipality to the neighboring city of Marikina and the rest of Metropolitan Manila. This way, the road lays emblematic of the attitude of the town with regard to the rapid urban developments taking place: to widen the road would only obviously mean the town's willingness to welcome progress, and so cutting down these old trees was a price our town can only be too inclined to pay if it is to clearly demonstrate its tenacity for growth. The town, in other words, had to literally give way to these developments, or so it was how it was made felt to the people, and the town also had to make itself appear most eager for these changes; and so the town—my town—did what it did, which of course is not what it necessarily had to do but still chose to do anyway. Hence, all the sudden sunlight: the once canopied road was abruptly made exposed, which brings with it a certain hollowness that is more than the literal bareness now of the highway. Years later, in some spots where the old narra trees used to stand, what remains now are only stubborn stumps, rooted but dead, but still alive, as I would like to still think, in the way that they seem to continue to refuse the road from becoming completely flat.

When the shopping mall tries to delude people—and perhaps, to an extent, itself—that it primarily takes its "inspiration from nature," it does not mean that its own structure adapts to or mimics the surroundings; the building, after all, does not meld itself with the environment and hardly aspires to, if the "shaded array of green hues" on its façade—which appear gray to my eyes anyway most of the time—is any indication. Of course, little landscapes line the entrance and the way to the parking lot at the back of the mall, expectedly filled with ornamental palms and other shrubs. But these plants are always only kept up to a certain shape and a certain height, barely living up to the trees that once stood on these grounds: the duhats and the mangoes, the coconuts and the santols, the ipils and the talisays, and all the others I can scarcely recall now. The ipomea that the mall has been letting creep on the trellises at the back of the building, supposedly decorating the otherwise cold and dreary parking lot, does not exude the same tenacity of the wild grass that once covered the open field beside my former school—the wild grass whose seeds would gently float through the warm afternoon breeze, the seeds to which one of us might have uncannily wished at some point, in our childhood whim, that a mall be built in our town.

Once I chanced upon a classmate in the mall, right in front of Starbucks, after one of my usual visits to the town's small secondhand bookstore. John Stephen used to be seated beside me most of the time since grade school, but John Stephen and I have never talked to each other after graduating high school. I had been more engulfed in the nearby cities of Marikina and Quezon, while John Stephen, after finishing a vocational course in Marikina, eventually settled in our town; he would be often seen walking around the mall, said to be looking for work, while I would be hardly seen even by my childhood friends in my neighborhood because of work. In that one rare instance we met, John Stephen, in an attempt to make conversations and perhaps strike an affinity after all these years, awkwardly told me that where we were standing at that moment must be where the "stage" used to be. John Stephen was pertaining to the small roofed platform of what used to be our school, where we used to do countless recognition ceremonies and attempts at performances. It was barely a stage, of course, as small as our school really was, but the couple of trees at the back and the shrubs and ferns at the side and in front were enough to mark it as a space to watch. The palmeras, for one, were never dead—that is, until the land owner decided it was time for our school to go elsewhere and sold the place to the supermall chain. Construction of the establishment began in 2014, and the mall opened a year later as the 52nd branch of the supermall brand in the country; our school, meanwhile, moved to another location, to a different barangay in our town, in a land whose title is now its own. To date, however, our school has never quite managed to regrow a verdure on par with its previous landscape.

The only testament to the school's previous location that is easily searchable online is this: barely a mention in the Wikipedia page of SM City San Mateo that says, "A fraction of the mall site was the former site of a school… which has then transferred to Brgy. Sta. Ana…" No picture of the old greenery seems to be readily available on the internet. And so, at times now, it feels like a fever dream to even remember the sound of a lone santol falling and hitting the roof of our classroom at the first two quarters of the school year or the duhats staining the ground at the final quarter (the mangoes, meanwhile, we seem to have never chanced upon; after all, the trees would usually fruit during our vacation in the old school calendar—from March to June). These little things—the rustling of the leaves, the crunching of the leaves, the smell of the leaves—all of these things feel farther and farther the older I get, as one is wont after all, but the more my town changes, progresses, develops, advances, modernizes, grows…—the more my town *changes*, the more impossible these sensations also seem from actually having happened before. I barely see any fruiting trees now in my town, and moreso during their actual fruition. One can easily say, of course, that the remaining trees might just be having difficulties bearing fruits nowadays, thinking how their vigor might be stunted now by all the changes that the town's soil as a whole is experiencing. But at the same time, I could not help but blame myself, too, for my own absence: more and more, I was simply not there—in my own town—to witness anything.

And so, in turn, the more and more I also have to rely on my own memory, if only to persist that once there was a time when instead of this present "green" shoe box of a shopping mall (SM, after all, originally stands for "Shoe Mart"), an assortment of flora truly grew from this very ground. I remember and choose to do so in order for the thicket to remain real, even if only in a time completely past in my head. Whenever I visit the mall and see a plantbox or a pot ornamented with plastic plants—plastic palms, plastic shrubs, plastic flowers, and even plastic grass—what I see in my mind's eye are the ghosts of plants that pervaded the place before. I imagine where these plants once grew and what they could have been now had the field remained, or at least had a chance to remain, as it was. It is a sight that, as I would like to believe, is not quite pastoral. I imagine parts of these plants rustling in the breeze, but I also imagine parts of them already bitten by insects that lived among them, although often unseen. I imagine these plants entangled with each other, jostling each other for sunlight, and so I imagine some parts of them, too, turning crisp and brown because they were ultimately left untouched by sunlight. I imagine years of quiet, years and years of stillness, their years of being alive that I—or anyone, for that matter—never quite witnessed. I imagine all the things I did not see, hear, or feel, but I knew happened anyway in that seemingly motionless piece of land that is now gone. I imagine some of the plants silently dying there over time, if only to imagine them eventually nourishing the same earth again and then slowly turning back to become other plants, different plants, by way of their decayed nutrient selves. I imagine all of these little tender lives—they who practically never die.

Aristotle considers the plant as possessing a soul, one that is always carefully predicated by the categorization of merely "vegetal." In his taxonomy, this means it is a soul that has the capacity to grow and to procreate but does not share the ability of "animal" souls to sense and to move and of "human" souls to think and to reason. In this sense, vegetal souls are at the lowest rung in the Aristotelian hierarchy, as they are said to only *seem* to live. What

Aristotle was not able to conceive at the time, however, was how movement and even reason can be rethought in terms that are beyond the human: when nearby trees send out signals to each other underground, what we can see now is a telegraphic intelligence that is, in some ways, more advanced than human telecommunications. Or when seeds scatter themselves through wind or other matters and plant themselves in a different piece of land—isn't this, too, a form of walking, albeit one that takes time and thus patience, which is more than the animal or even the human soul can bear? All in all, Aristotle, it can be said now, missed a lot. Plants, of course, are as alive as animals and humans; it is only a shame that it took us a long time to relearn what ancient myths have already taught us.

I, for one, know that plant souls are as potent, if not more, because they are souls that persist even after their physical bodies have been long gone; they linger, for one, in our minds, just as how plants we ordinarily eat shape how we think, how we move, and how we feel. In Rizal's *Noli me tángere*, for instance, the protagonist Ibarra once saw ghosts of plants: as he looks out from his carriage and to a nineteenth-century botanical garden in Manila, what he saw instead were the gardens of Europe, where, as he sadly remembers, plants are carefully tended, made to bear flowers despite the high costs of doing so, given the often inhospitable climate. Rizal, of course, was drawing a metaphor for the colonial condition of the country under Spanish rule: the Philippines is such an uncultivated garden, simply left to wither, despite the fact that plants are supposed to grow and bloom easier in the tropical parts of the world; even the talisays—the tropical almonds—native to the country, as they were described, continue to be thin, emaciated, and stunted ("Los almendros... no habían crecido, continuaban raquíticos"), which can only suggest a degradation of the soil at the time, given the rapid developments happening in Manila. What Rizal names then in the novel as "el demonio de las comparaciones" might as well be a demon that is really the ghosts of plants: the diabolic sensation which, according to Benedict Anderson, makes it virtually impossible for one to experience Europe without thinking about Manila, and vice versa—what could it be but the trace of all the plant souls now lost, yet remaining here on earth, insisting to be recognized, too, amid all the transformations happening in the present.

Unlike Rizal, however, who was fortunate enough to have the figure of Europe to turn to, whenever I am haunted by these ghosts of plants, I only have my memory to see them through the other side of time—memory that is, at best, contentious: was the field as big and as full as my mind remembers it to be? Was it really as green as I make it seem to be now, in this prose? Did fire trees actually stand there as well, or am I conflating the image of red-on-green with another place, with another verdure, given the commonality of these plants in the tropics? The uncertain remembrances, in a way, only make it apparent for me that the field I once knew is a kind of wound now, too. Of course, they might simply be the consequence of me not paying attention to my surroundings while growing up, but precisely the fact that I was not able to anticipate my town harshly changing the way it did is what especially hurts. There is loss somewhere here, and it is a loss that is more unnameable and innumerable than usual because how does one—or, how can one ever—grieve over, say, a patch of overgrown? There is loss somewhere; this I can very much feel, despite the fact that I am not also quite sure what the shape of this absence I carry within. What, after all, is the silhouette of a thicket, *this* thicket? And more so, of a thicket that I did not really spend a lot of time in, only encountered from a certain distance, safely passed by?

And if one does not know the shape of absence that they say they somehow carry, do they actually carry such a lack within? Or is it simply a specter of hollowness, a phantom of emptiness? A sad ghost of a feeling? Writing it all down, if only to further probe this haunting of a lack, can only balm so much. Time feels irreversible and *is* irreversible, at least for now. But somehow, this, too, must be taken as a gift for the comfort it oddly offers: that an SM mall stands less than a kilometer away from my house, right where my old school used to be—does this not also mean a sooner oblivion? The road to progress, after all, as Walter Benjamin paints it, is one that always and inevitably discards itself, making mountains out of debris. And so, several years from now, vines will creep on the walls of this mall, and not just on the trellis it has previously designated. The concrete will be covered in moss. Wild plants will take over.

JONATHAN CHAN

*blue*_____

are the skies, furnished with
the pink undersides of passing
clouds, refracted, warped
by the cloying shade of plastic
recycle bins. no space for
intransigent language: grue
or wine-red in a spectrum
of daily churning. blue is the
sweat across a bottle of Soju
from Jeju, or the threads around
a hole on an old Nike t-shirt, or
the dust shaken from a pair
of running shoes. blue are
the garish pixels on tired eyes,
the whiplash of news, blue
adorning folded planes and
stolid fonts. blue the color of
hyperlinkage, highlights, unfurling
filaments of a leather case. its
innards crackle with an electric
surge; blue winnowed from
mineral, sea, and air.

MARK ANGELES

Hut in a Bottle

People call him *bunso*—
The youngest
In the dorm of gang members,
Not by age, but by last entry
Behind bars for stealing
From his boss his unpaid salary.

In the workshop, he sat
Beside those whose toothbrushes
Turn into ice picks,
Who weave bags and frames
Using drinking straws and beads.
Today, they make nipa houses

Inside gin bottles.
Steady hands glued *banig*
Into bamboo frames, crowned it
With a thatch of *pawid*.
His handiwork became the subject
Of cross examination.

A snow globe of sorts,
His nipa hut was submerged
In muddy flood. Who'll buy such?
We have enough storm warnings.
—A memento, he quipped,
Of my village that sinks

During high tide, with water
That holds out for weeks;

Even with clear skies. The seas
Barge into our doorsteps.
Like mad dogs, they watch us
Move on with our lives.

நீங்கள் எதை இழந்தீர்கள்?

(What Did You Lose?)

To my great-grandfather, Munusamy, who was among the Malayan Tamil laborers pronounced missing during the construction of the Death Railway (Burma-Siam Railway). It is rumored that he was tortured to death by Japanese soldiers for faking an attendance on behalf of a fellow laborer who contracted Cholera.

If memory is the only casket accorded to you
and I may well be the last bearer,
then tell me, how would you like this story told?
Shall I soften the tragedy?

Perhaps the sky pouted
with the arrival of indolent dusk
and the wind whistled an aching lullaby.
Perhaps when your eyes glazed over,
the last glint on the track bed
looked like கோலிக்குண்டு[1]
and you could almost hear
the marbles your daughters played with
clang and clatter in the distance.

For a moment, you could forget
the pale greys of jutting quarried stones
and how blood splatters and dries
into ugly browns between the incisors.
For a moment, your world was green again,
shaded by high branching limbs,
and tree barks that bled
milky white like a new mother.

உங்கள் இழப்புகளால்
இந்த நிலம் என்ன பெற்றது?²
பயிர் விதைப்பதற்குப் பதிலாக
ரயில் விதைத்தீர்கள்.³

The steel you carried on your back
in place of the daughters you couldn't—
did they also whimper
through the nightmare of your absence?
Perhaps somewhere in Siam, even today,
when the bolts unclench to rest,
they still taste the rust of your blood
between their molars.

Did you know you'd never make it home?
Shall I write that you cried
into the water there for months
and hoped the salt turned into sea elsewhere—
and how that very hope mothered you
through the smothering heat and disease?
Or will running water break
the suspension of disbelief?

Perhaps death was a courteous guest
that didn't overstay his welcome;
a hammer to the head,
a bayonet to the chest,
or simply thrown half-alive
into a pit of fire?

If no bodies were recovered,
you are a nobody.
If thousands of bodies were recovered,
you are still a nobody.
Who are you amongst a hundred thousand?
Just a sheaf of grass uprooted
and cast aside by a careless fist.
But here we are, the rest of you,
seeds sprouted from the same weed
scattered across lands.

உங்கள் இழப்புகளால்
நான் என்ன அடைந்தேன்?⁴

After a better part of a century,
my tongue—swollen
from the sorrows you swallowed,
blistered and forever unquenched—
struggles against the chokehold
of your stories.

The roof of my mouth tries to house you,
to beckon you home.
You whom I've never met,
you whom my mother has never met,
you whom my mother's mother could only bury
in the back of her mind.

Tell me, who's going to console your motherland
when she demands answers about her missing sons?
Has she always known you'd never make it home?
Or has she also forgotten?

If memory is the only casket accorded to you,
and I'm the last remaining bearer,
then tell me, how shall I lay you down?

NOTES

1. Goli gundu—a traditional Indian street game of flicking marbles into a hole.

2. What was born of this land from your losses?

3. Instead of seeds, you sowed railway tracks.

4. What did I gain from your losses?

DIANA RAHIM

The Restoration

Zubaidah knew, as anyone who has ever tried to bury a body, how hard it is to break through soil. Two years ago, she carried and laid the body of her deceased cat, Lontong, gently on the grass before attempting to dig up a chosen plot of soil. She did so, absurdly, with a steel spatula.

Perhaps it was something about the soil here. Repeatedly, her steel spatula hit the hard surface uselessly. The ground remained determinedly unbreached. Her heart, already so ravaged by the specific grief of losing a pet, felt itself fully undone. A soft thing, a sandcastle dissolved unthinkingly by the banal hand of an ocean.

People walked past, seemingly cold, but in truth they too felt themselves helplessly mournful at the sight of Zubaidah, with her one hand stroking Lontong's already stiffening body and the other holding up the edges of her hijab to her eyes as she cried. They clutched their packed dinners, laptop bags, and the hands of their children a little tighter as they turned their eyes away from the disarmingly intimate sight of her grief and walked home in a waning evening.

It made sense why there were tractors at the Muslim graveyards scooping up massive mounds of soil. She had found their presence loathsome and vulgar at her daughter's burial six years ago, but understood then that even the earth struggles to accept the death of its children.

Zubaidah knew better now. When she decided that she wanted to plant trees, she immediately identified the open field behind the clump of neighborhoods she lived in as the best place. The field had been cleared many decades ago, and the other half of the forest it once belonged to remained untouched and feral. All she would have to do was plant trees furtively along their naked edge, and she was confident that nobody would notice.

The first tree she wanted to plant was a rain tree. *Pukul Lima.* Five o'clock. That's what the tree was called in her tongue. Named after the time at which the tree's leaves would fold up at the sunset hour.

Of course, sunset was no longer at five o'clock. Not since the 80s, when the land's standard time was moved forward. Now they no longer shared the same time as Batam, which was just about an hour away by boat, but shared the same time as Hong Kong, Beijing, and Perth. How mutable time seemed.

64

How deceptive the human's seeming power. They changed these things and left the trees alienated from the meaning of their names.

Zubaidah knew she had to wait for the yellow pods to turn brown, signaling the ripening of the seeds inside. She waited patiently. Throughout the island, they followed a seemingly singular rhythm. The day she finally could get the seeds was the day she visited her daughter's grave. She had bid her daughter her customary farewell first.

Mak go home first ok Syimah, I'll visit you again next week.

She noticed on the walk away from the graveyard the difference in the rain trees by the path of the road. She gathered the brown pods on the soft ground of the earth, wondering, as she gathered them, whether unmarked bodies rested and gave themself to the growth of the tree. When she arrived home, she split open the pods to gather the seeds.

Was it wise to plant a rain tree in a field? She did not know. She never really had a green thumb, nor had she tended to more than a few plants in her life. All of them had died under her care, not out of negligence but due to varying reasons of overabundance. Shifting one plant to where the sun shone brightest, it would eventually shrivel from direct heat. Another would die from too much watering. Zubaidah did not know how to moderate her giving. She did not know that there could be such a thing as too much love.

*

She would cook their meals, and they would eat separately. That is the way it has been the past two years with Zubaidah and her husband. If you were to ask her about it, she would be silent with the realization that she had never considered the distance.

Despite their distance, her responsibility to him (and his to her) remained and took up the time in their lives. She did the laundry, went to the market, and prepared the food. He would work, do the dishes, and sweep the floor. But once a week, she has time to herself to spend purely alone. Those are the Tuesdays she visits their daughter's grave.

Her husband does not wish to go, and Zubaidah does not press him. He had cried the day of their daughter's funeral so inconsolably that she did not feel free to cry herself. He was almost wailing—a broken radio of despair. Unnerving and urgent as a siren. *Hasyimah, my child. Hasyimah, my child.*

It felt as if there was an allotted amount of expression allowed, and he had taken it all for himself. She did not fault him for this. She could not. Especially after she heard her brother console him terribly by saying, *Calm down, make peace with reality. You're crying like a woman.*

Still, sometimes when she sits by her daughter's grave to talk to her and offer prayers, when she wipes down the tombstone, when she waters the soil, and on special occasions when she scatters a potpourri of flowers, she wishes she had another body to lean on as she feels her sorrow unspooling from a tight place deep inside her being. This place always smelled of fresh soil, bleached cotton, and rose water.

Once, she had thought to herself that she understood why some Chinese people left cooked food for their deceased. It would be a consolation to still practice these loving rituals for your loved one. To still believe that they could be nourished by your labor. You could still give something to them after all this time, and they would receive it, even if it was in a form you did not understand. The first person to have done that must have been a grieving mother.

The first time she went to bury the seeds, she left on a Tuesday morning after performing her subuh prayers. The sun had yet to rise when she left, and she opened the door to the smell of dusk and sleep. She walked the ten minutes to reach the open field, walking all the way to the edge of the forest at the point where the field began. The line of trees stood like sentinels, the first line of defense from any future violation.

Reaching into her bag, she unscrewed the cap from her bottle of water and poured it on the soil to soften it. With a spade, she dug a broad, shallow space, being careful to dig just the right depth—too deep and the seed would struggle to push through; too shallow and it would be vulnerable to the elements. The only good thing that had been done through the decimation of the forest was that they had leveled the land so that the soil was even. This made things easier for her. Dropping the seeds inside and covering them with soil, she watered the spot again. Not too much this time.

She did this week after week for a full month, always being careful to space out the distance between the seeds. She would plant a seed, then head to the graveyard to visit her daughter. When her fiftieth birthday arrived, she realized that once a week was much too slow for her to repopulate that field to its full strength.

She decided, unreasonably, that she must plant a seed every day.

*

"This is where my kampung used to be. And all of this space used to be filled with trees. When I get off the train station you could see trees all around you. There used to be only one main road in Sembawang, and the road is still there. All of these roads weren't here, not even our neighborhood existed. Can you imagine?"

Once in a while, Zubaidah told her daughter iterations of this speech during their peaceful walks home as they passed the forest. Sometimes her daughter listened to her, sometimes not, and sometimes her daughter would talk over her, ensnared with the excitement of yet another thing that was consuming her world at that moment. Hasyimah had been a rambunctious talker, rattling off about wanting to go to the playground, asking Zubaidah for the names of plants, complaining about classmates, or requesting twenty times in a row if please, could Mak *please* have McDonald's for lunch?

In her memories, she remembered these moments with Hasyimah when she was five, then eight, then twelve. Her daughter rose in height and voice and then disappeared as Zubaidah was brought back to the present.

When half of that forest was cut down, it felt like she had to grieve another kind of death. As if she was being denied even the comfort that spatial consistency brings; as if the distance from memory had widened. Now she didn't just have to remember her walks with her daughter; she also had to do the job of remembering the forest. She was twice removed.

Just the same, as she aged, it felt as if she were being denied the memory of her childhood when forests were obliterated to make way for new roads, neighborhoods, and malls. She would end up living in a unit in one of those neighborhoods herself. She had been living in the same place her whole life, but time and again, she had been displaced.

It was the vertigo of staying in place while being simultaneously uprooted.

Zubaidah may not have had a green thumb, but she had a long memory. She remembered what the land looked like, the trees that self-sufficiently existed without knowledge of their impending deaths, their names, the sight of birds and their nests resting on the branches, cats slinking into the forests in search of medicinal plants to cure bruised bellies, and even lovers seeking privacy under dense canopies.

So she knew, without having to read too much, that a forest that was fully alive was not manicured but a lush experience. The trees would vary in height, and plants would be softly erupting from the ground. A forest had to be left to itself, for it knows its own needs best. Walking past manicured gardens in her neighborhood, especially in those areas that were neglected, gave her a feeling of distress, as if the plants were communicating to her that they were in prison and in pain. Walk into a forest that had been left on its own, and you could immediately feel the difference. The energy was one of primal self-sufficiency, and you felt yourself as a small being, a visitor. A forest, unlike a quaint garden, possessed a dignity that was almost terrifying.

For now, though, she was staging an intervention. There was no guarantee that she could replicate the energy and the full needs of the forest through her daily seeding, but she knew she just had to do this for long enough until the forest would take over.

After a month, however, none of the seeds she had planted had even sprouted. The first week that she decided to go every day, she felt herself drained as she was met with failure after failure.

At the end of the week, returning with an aching back and her heavy bag of utensils, her husband was waiting for her on the sofa.

"Where were you?"

"I was out…"

"You have been coming back late every day, where do you go exactly?"

"I went to do the groceries." Zubaidah felt herself sinking into her lie, suddenly overcome with the fear of a teenager being accosted by parents and the realization that she had not heard her husband talk to her beyond the basic pleasantries for years.

"Then where are your groceries?"

Her husband was visibly confused. She could see that he even seemed a little scared.

Zubaidah searched for something to say as her husband entertained terrible thoughts.

"Have you been seeing another man?" he asked, his voice shuddering with a fragility that was so quintessentially him, the very essence of his softness, a quality that had endeared him to her decades ago, its rare quality dulled through the normalization of decades of domestic life.

"Eh! Of course not!" Zubaidah yelled. Then, as if a weight had dropped off her shoulders, she laughed.

"At my age, abang? How to see another man? What would we do? Go to the market together?"

But her husband was in his space of fragility and would not be so easily appeased by her lighthearted humor. Sulking, he asked again where her groceries were.

She passed him her bag and sat on the sofa.

"There, my groceries." She smiled.

He held up a spade and stared questioningly at the dirt. She explained everything.

Some days later, her husband came home with three saplings, a shovel and a declaration that he would follow her into the field.

*

When she could not bury Lontong two years ago, she googled the words "bury pet Singapore" and came across the company "Heaven 4 Pets," which offered cremation and even columbarium services. The cheapest option was communal cremation, where many animals were cremated at the same time, and the ashes, all commingled together, would not be returned to the owner but scattered elsewhere. "To the sea," they had said, but Zubaidah suspected that was a polite way of hiding more convenient methods of disposal.

She would have preferred to have a "private cremation," where Lontong would be cremated alone and she would have the room to herself, but it would cost her an exorbitant $600. In the end, she picked "individual cremation," which cost $300. Lontong would be cremated along with another pet while separated by a screen, and she would be able to bring his ashes home in an urn. It was still expensive, but she knew her husband would not protest, since he had not come with her to the crematorium or helped settle anything else related to Lontong's death.

That day, the workers had kindly laid Lontong on the metal tray, surrounded by an assortment of flowers. It was a gentle sight, and Zubaidah took it upon herself to rearrange some of the carnations. She then pulled out an old blouse of hers and laid it on top of his body as if it were a blanket. She took pictures, which she planned to later print at a photo shop and put in a small frame at her bedside. She performed all of these steps slowly, with restrained calm, aware that her whole body was tense with the energy of grief, even anger. Loss, again. To deal with its practicalities alone, again.

As Lontong's body was pulled into the fire, she felt an explosion of protectiveness and shame. How could she have allowed this to happen? How could she be letting his body burn? One of the workers who had brought Lontong's body in had lingered, even though they were supposed to give customers privacy. She could see Zubaidah's breathing grow frantic. It was not easy for those who came to the crematorium alone. She approached quietly, gave Zubaidah a kindly rub on her shoulders in consolation, and looked into Zubaidah's tearful eyes with an understanding smile.

"Your cat so cute Mak Cik, what was their name?"

"Lontong," Zubaidah replied, bringing her hijab to dab her tears and worrying if her blood pressure was being aggravated.

"That's the cutest name I've heard for a cat! And I've been working here for five years." The worker laughed.

Zubaidah managed a pained smile and tried to breathe deeply.

"My daughter gave him the name. He used to live on our block. Whenever my daughter was walking home, he would follow her all the way home, right up to our gate. He only did that with her. With other people, he would just keep sleeping."

Zubaidah looked at the flames and felt herself getting calmer.

"My daughter used to say, 'Mak, this cat white color like Lontong!' At her tenth birthday party, Lontong actually came to our house! It was so funny, I tell you. My husband told my daughter, "Syimah, your best friend is here to see you!" and everyone kept laughing because we were so noisy and excited, but Lontong was just sitting in front of the gate very politely. Really *very* funny!"

Zubaidah laughed, and the worker was laughing too.

"But I also felt like it was a miracle. Like he wanted to wish her happy birthday. Or maybe he just memorized the route to our house; I don't know."

"I think it's a miracle," the worker replied assuredly.

Beyond the partition, Zubaidah could hear another person crying, and she wondered if they heard her laughing.

"How old is your daughter?" The worker asked.

"twelve years old."

It was the same answer she had given for the past six years.

"We're so lucky to have cats, right, Mak Cik? Not everyone gets to know how special it is to love a cat and for them to love us. But we know."

Zubaidah decided to bring along the urn containing Lontong's ashes one day as they marched into the field so she could pour it on the bed of soil of a sapling. As she patted down the soil of the sapling, now forever interred with

Lontong's ashes, she finally found herself agreeing with what the worker said two years ago. She felt lucky to have had Lontong and to have seen her daughter interact with him. She cried copiously, overcome with the relief of giving him the kind of rest she felt all beings wanted—a return to the earth.

She patted down the soil lovingly, not entirely sure why she was doing so. She was simply moving as she intuitively felt guided to. Her husband had plucked a bunch of ixora flowers from a nearby bush and placed them on the soil.

"Syimah's best friend," he said, smiling.

"If only we can do the same with Syimah," Zubaidah said.

Her husband turned his eyes away from the ixoras and toward her.

"Well, right now she is sharing a grave with eight other people, so we can only wait when her grave gets *en bloc-ed* in another nine years! When we claim her remains, we can bring her and maybe even her friends here," he replied, entertaining his wife's fancy.

"How can you joke about Syimah's grave like that?" Zubaidah yelped. It was mock horror, he knew, for even as she was turning to walk away, he could hear her laughing.

*

Zubaidah had received the idea from a video she saw about an Indian man named Jadav Payeng. He had planted a tree every day for thirty years to save a forest that had diminished by half and was facing the possibility of being completely submerged. The government had initially planned reforesting efforts but had abandoned them halfway. In the video she saw, Jadav Payeng was wearing pants and a white shirt tucked in. She thought it was a rather troublesome get-up to wear when you were about to go into a forest and plant trees, but realized she would probably dress smartly if someone were to film her for a documentary too. For Jadav Payeng's forest, there were trees like Arjun, Pride of India, royal poinciana, moj, and cotton trees. Because of him, wildlife had returned to the forest. A herd of 100 elephants would spend six months every year in the forest, even birthing their calves there.

If I were to do this, Zubaidah had thought, I would have palm trees, pukul lima, angsana, meranti, pulai, and ketapang, and why not even plant some bunga telang, ulam raja, daun kesum, and cili padi? It would be so convenient to pluck what she needed instead of buying them from the market. In fact, it would be a good idea to plant a kapok tree. She could use their fiber to stuff pillows and mattresses, just like in the good old times. Her mother had even used it to clean Zubaidah's bum as a baby—a traditional wet wipe. She lost herself in thinking of her own forest and what animals might return if she could do what Jadav Payeng did.

When her husband announced that he wanted to follow her into the field, the first thing she did was show him the video.

"Doesn't he look so kind? You can tell, even if we didn't know he was planting trees. It's because of the way he talks. My grandmother used to talk like this, very gently," she had said. Jadav Payeng was describing the trees that would help hold the soil and prevent erosion.

"I think you speak like this too. Just like him," her husband had replied, factually and without sentiment. They had watched the rest of the video in silence.

Zubaidah stopped visiting her daughter's grave after she decided to plant a seed each day. But each day that she went into the field, she felt her daughter's presence. She felt closer to her than any time she had sat by the grave. In fact, Zubaidah would replicate the rituals in the graveyard as she tended to the trees.

As she approached the field, she would brightly announce her arrival, *Syimah, Mak is here to see you.*

Her husband held back his tears when he heard her say that for the first time, almost tripping even though they were walking on even ground. Somehow, her behavior did not strike him as irrational. He was used to her earthly, unexplainable, and unique form of spiritualism.

She poured the water on the soil with the same care as she had poured water on her daughter's grave. She even offered a prayer after the planting of a seed or sapling.

The first morning he joined her on the field, he had spent much time loosening as much soil as he could to begin the work of amending it. He would have to do this each day as they go, he told her, making sure to add a layer of leaves to improve the texture and ensure that there were enough nutrients for the soil. She had been overcome with anger when he explained this. How laborious it was to ensure a thing could grow, and how easily these things could die.

He then planted three saplings densely together in the space of a square meter.

"We need to make up for the last month," he said, not unkindly.

Those first three trees were meranti trees. They were capable of growing tall, reaching the status of the highest level of the canopy of a forest.

"Let's plant a banana tree next; every forest needs some fruit trees. We can plant some mango trees in the future also," he said as they walked back.

"We will only need to do this for two years. Plant the trees, pull out any weeds, water the field. After two years, the forest will take care of itself. Two years, then we will stop, okay?" he added.

Zubaidah did not reply, choosing instead to bid her customary farewell. *Syimah, Mak, and Ayah go home first; we'll come back again soon.*

Clay

The woman has never felt herself
this full of earth. Her hands

have unearthed a scent as old
as the first rains. She has

a basket, a trowel and hard fingers
with which to dig from a vein

under the skin of soil. She scoops
its fruit, soft and rich,

the color of afterbirth
just after. It sits in her basket, naked.

Hoisted, is the weight of a year-old him.
At home, the woman slakes its thirst

with water. Wetted, fed with rice
chaff, stroked and kneaded, it blinks

and takes shape—a mouth, a neck,
ribs, a body to fit the circle of arms.

The woman wonders at its yielding, soft
as a newborn's suckle, and as fierce.

With a seashell, she combs
in its flesh waves she imagines it must

once have known. For they say the river
here was once the sea. That the sea

is a mother. The woman wonders
at the sea's mothering: her infinite

indifference. Her swallowing of sons.
The woman places it in the safety of shade.

In the lace of shadows, lingers.
By the seventh sunrise, it is dry.

She knows it must now be placed
in the bidding fire. But she cannot do it.

She will hold it for a while more in its
newness, before its hardening.

Before, like him, it too is carried
off like a song on saltwind.

Con cò bé bé, nó đậu cành tre,
Đi không hỏi mẹ, biết đi đường nào[1]

She looks at her hands
and wonders at the redness of earth.

NOTES

1. From Vietnamese nursery rhyme "Mẹ Yêu Không Nào (Con Cò Bé Bé)."
    Roughly translates into "Little baby stork on a bamboo branch went away with-
    out asking mum. She doesn't know where it went."

Sumbawa[1]

Mataram, 2022

when the eastern sun creeps over the sea
roots hold the ancient secrets of trees
they know this rainy season belongs to agarwood
but the distance of the leaves is getting farther away
let the wind sweep their fallen feeling;
yellow, red, brown, like sincerity of all time

tambora[2] stares from its height
cranes in the middle of a misty field
fly like the old farmers
when they face the endless sky
their echo sounds like a pain

rain falls on the black foot of the hill
the road is like a distant past
the sappan[3] forest is starting to peel
the current is getting stronger

NOTES

1. Sumbawa is an island in the south-eastern part of Indonesia.

2. Tambora, a volcano in Sumbawa Island, erupted in 1815.

3. Sappan (Indonesia, sepang) is a trade commodity, most popular in the colonial era.

Coat Buttons

They've stopped cutting the grass. In other words, they've stopped beheading the coat buttons. These days, I see more bees than ever, weaving in and out of the thin stems, alighting on one flower, then the next.

*

The way a child learns disappointment is to pick up the white fluffy fruiting body of the coat button, huff and puff, and realize that it will never disperse in the wind the way dandelions do in the stories.

*

I once watched my grandmother hold the finest needles in her mouth and fix the fraying thread with her spit before mending her softest shirts. When reinforcing buttons, I've found no way to pull the thread through, except to force the needle in and snatch it back as it nicks the epidermal layer of my skin.

*

With the little bees, I am fairly certain about the single-use nature of their stings.

*

As a child, I thought of the coat buttons as false daisies. How the protruding yellow center with its pockmarks and the white petals, with their tooth-like edges, resembled a textbook daisy had it been thrown into the washer, wrung, then tumbled dry on high heat.

*

When stabbed by a needle, I pinch the wound until it no longer draws blood. Perhaps hold my breath and play dead—the rest is muscle memory.

*

To this day, I do not know if I am allergic to the stings of the yellow jacket, showing up for dinner when the grilled meat is served: salted, lightly charred, fat dripping.

*

To test the fiber content of fabric, you have to burn it. Alternatively, you may read the label to predict if the soft silk-like shirt you are wearing will blaze, then cool into a lump of hard plastic.

*

In an anaphylactic shock caused by a bee sting, it is necessary to seek immediate medical attention and remove the offending stinger. If the stinger is visible, one may press a credit card against the skin where it shows and gently coax it out. Avoid the use of tweezers, which may break the stinger and trap it further beneath the skin.

*

Something about fire will drive the bees away. Incense, the flicker of a light, cigarette smoke, cremation. Still, the coat buttons will cluster two days after the mowing begins again, as though falling out of a grass cutter's pocket.

IAN NIEVERO JEREZ

A Symphony of Waves

I

Since he was a child, Timothy Salazar knew he was peculiar.

His parents thought he was unremarkable—a one-dimensional boy, a soul lacking depth. As a child, he never stepped outside the perimeters of his room unless his mother checked on him every two hours or announced breakfast, lunch, or dinner once it was served on the dining table. His parents never bothered to ask themselves about what transpired inside his room. Not that there was any funny business inside his room, but his parents valued his personal space. They never went inside his room. The closest thing they did to entering his room was to stand by the door after they knocked. His parents believed that even a child like him deserved the privacy that adults always demanded from children.

When his parents took him to the beach one summer at their hometown in Cavite, the sight of cerulean waves terrified him, and with anything that terrified him, he wanted to move closer to it, to scrutinize it, to explore it not only with his hands but also with his entire body, to touch the very source of his fears. The waves rhythmically crashed onto the shore, dampening the sand, and slinked its way back into bigger bodies of water, into that extensive line where the azure touched the sea.

He wanted to touch that line.

While his mom lost sight of him, he was possessed by an arbitrary idea: to take a swim. The waters spoke to him the way all fearful objects did to him. He tread his way beyond the shoreline and toward the water, his feet maintaining their balance. The water began to rise—from his ankles to his knees, to his torso, to his chest, then up to his neck—as he walked deeper into it, the line marking the point between the skies and the waters getting closer as he continued his pace. When his body was submerged in the water, what he expected was the usual sensation of drowning, but his body felt none of that; rather, it responded to the water. His legs lifted effortlessly behind him. The water found its way inside his body, and he sank further into the water, which felt like air. His body moved and slowly made a dive.

He continued to swim and opened his eyes; something came into full view, a few meters away from where he was, the current of the waves leaving him unbothered. He saw the face of a woman or a man, an exposed torso, and, to his astonishment, a tail twirling from behind. The creature made its way in his direction, swimming rapidly, its tail swinging and quivering, coming closer.

He heard an animalistic howl, which he definitely knew came from his mother, back from the shoreline, and the thunderous, collective cries of *help-help-help!* from strangers, tourists, and families who witnessed everything.

Then his body was lifted from the water by the male lifeguard in swimming trunks. He held him in his arms and carried him back to the shoreline.

"What were you thinking?" His mother shrieked at him, slapping him hard across the face.

"I wanted to touch the water," he said to his mother.

The more his parents advised him not to do anything again, the more he wanted to do those things. He took the proverb, "Curiosity killed the cat," to a whole new level of interpretation that drove his parents into a state of paranoia. Ever since the occurrence at the beach, they regularly visited him in his room, but they didn't find anything suspicious.

All Timothy Salazar knew was that what he saw underneath the waters made his skin crawl, just like all things that he feared.

II

When he was twelve, he and his Ninong Pio entered a toy retail store on the ground floor of the mall. He entered an aisle in glossy pink, flanked by dolls in various sizes, from the smallest on the bottom to the medium-sized on the middle, then to the largest on the top. He was in the girls' section, and he wasn't supposed to be here. Among the boxes consisting of miniature figurines dressed in exaggerated pastel dresses and with heads covered in humongous, vibrant wigs in shades of purple, pink, and red, his eyes were drawn by one figurine inside the store. A figure of such sublimity brought him into downright hypnosis, his eyes fixated on one body: a doll whose lower half was cloaked by an elongated fluke in dusky shades of blue, evocative of the smell of water, instead of the ordinary legs and feet of a female doll.

They were like no other to him—the dolls. When he reached his hand to stroke the doll's red hair—regardless of it being secured inside a box—he felt another person's hand swat his own hand away from the figurine, accountable for his state of hypnosis and for his abrupt, heightened focus.

Those dolls are not suited for you, his Ninong Pio explained to him. *You should be more interested on miniature cars and robots than those absurd dolls. Are you a girl?* He flinched at the tone of Ninong Pio's voice, which was rough and condescending. His ninong moved closer to the doll inside the box, his eyes glaring at the figure harshly and his eyebrows arched. To match his height with his godson, Ninong Pio kneeled before him and looked at him carefully.

You want to become a mermaid, Timmy?

The question alone confused him, but the idea that the question brought sparked his inquisitiveness and his sense of exploration. While he stood in the middle of the aisle lined by dolls, he visualized himself in the skin of a mermaid, the lower half of his body blanketed by a fluke consisting of the color and smell of the earth, his whole body perching on top of a rock, the fluke independently swaying and twirling in concert with the symphony of waves as they crashed against the solid surface of the earth, where he rested with his eyes closed, breathing in the air seeping through the pair of eggshells concealing his flat-chested breasts.

There was something both intriguing and strange about the doll as he finally pulled it out of its box inside his bedroom. Two cerulean seashells covered the mermaid's breasts. Her red hair effortlessly fell on the back of her neck, and the color of her scales was proportional to the seashells protecting her breasts. He ran his fingers through the mermaid's scales and fluked, marveling at their breathtaking sublimity. He had not seen something as exquisite as the mermaid he held delicately with his hands. Not even the mermaid portrayed by both television and folklore surpassed what his Ninong Pio had bought him.

For one strange minute, he heard a voice coming from the walls of his bedroom, from underneath the four corners of his bed, from every mirror he looked inside his home, from the discomfiting space of the closet by the wall near the window where the moonlight kissed the drawn curtains, whispering the same message from everywhere he looked inside his room.

Dive into me, Timothy. Dive into me.

He returned his gaze to the mermaid—a child's eyes looking through the creature's ocean-like eyes as they held his gaze, taking him in. He sensed something move against his hold on the creature—a rhythmic, graceful sway of its faux fluke and the grazing of its scales on his skin, enraptured by his clutch on its hips and by its newfound master.

III

The evening Timothy Salazar left Cavite for Manila, he didn't sleep and never found the will to sleep. A year had passed. He was thirteen when his mother drove him to her home in Manila, a city where a stranger like him didn't belong because of its intricacies, its self-absorbed citizens, its congested roads, its narrow, poorly constructed, and hostile sidewalks, its inaccessible transportation, unfavoring of the public, except for the rich, and mostly, the contaminated, oppressive air.

"He needs to recover from what happened," she reasoned out to his grandmother, who shook her head in disapproval and said that she had always been right from the start for not trusting that "*manyak*."

"You should never have allowed him into your home, Maita," his grandmother said while his mother settled her luggage beside the couch in the living room. He remained standing a few meters away from the front door.

"Ma, I didn't know it would even happen," his mother explained. "I didn't even know I could trust him until I came home." She stopped and glanced over at her son, who was staring at her and his grandmother.

"*You*"—his grandmother shoved a finger to his mother's chest—"should never have left him alone at home. You know *he*'s too friendly of a child." His grandmother glanced at him, her eyes inundated by unease, and looked back at his mother.

He went upstairs to the room where his mother advised him to stay. The room was just as spacious as his room at his home in Cavite. But what was home if it became the root of his terrors? He settled himself on the edge of the bed, took off his shoes, and placed them underneath the bed. It was already midnight, and he couldn't sleep. The heat withdrawn by the air conditioning had no effect on his body. Sweat moistened the back of his neck, his hair rising from his skin. On the bed, he curled and folded himself in a fetal position, his body hugging his knees. The comforter, which was crafted to give him comfort, faltered in translating the serenity he yearned for.

Timothy Salazar remembered the monthly evenings he had with Ninong Pio, who had accompanied him at home since he was alone every Friday, but his ninong had only visited once a month. Ninong Pio had explained to him that his parents weren't home from work yet; he had pulled out something from his bag—a *Goosebumps* book. Ninong Pio had handed him the copy.

How could such a book be complicit in his unexplainable rage against the continuing jolt of the hands on the flesh, unconsenting to be touched?

The shock of it all transpired when it was over. When he returned to his old room, he wondered what had gone wrong. Had it been wrong to say no in the presence of an adult? *It's bad to say no to adults, Timmy.* Ninong Pio had explained to him that since he had given him a new book to read, it was just fair that he received something in return.

After the remembering, he didn't sleep that night, and he could still hear the indefinite voices of his mother and grandmother downstairs. His eyes gazed at the darkness above him, the moonlight faintly streaming in from the windows, the sweat behind his neck trickling down to his back, dampening and staining the sheets and pillows, his arms clinging closely to his knees, as if he's holding on for dear life.

IV

Fifteen years after the shock his parents thought he had recovered from, he wants to come home to reclaim his homeland and its waters, unwilling to welcome him back.

When his father informs him of Ninong Pio's death, he requests a one-week leave, which his boss permits. Cardiac arrest, his father explains to him over the phone; his mother, on the other hand, can care any less about the news. Harvey Manansala, a longtime friend and partner of his, volunteers to drive him to Cavite, where the wake will take place. While they are on their way, with Harvey behind the wheel, he leans on the black, tinted window, where no sunlight streams in—nothing but the dampened glass steamed by the sudden downpour bulleting down from gray clouds, accompanied by thunder. The window is a barrier that is a distance between the outside world and his gaze, a contemplation of what-could-have-beens.

"I want to go back," he tells Harvey.

The room is on the second floor of the four-story hotel and resort overlooking Manila Bay and situated at the center of the municipality of Tanza in Cavite. Harvey taps the key card on the doorknob. The door unlocks itself with a clicking sound, and it slightly opens. Before he steps in, he senses the walls of the hallway closing in on him, its borders coercing him to step inside and lock himself in. That claustrophobic sense of isolation. It is such a peculiar thing how a place like this always takes him back, even if he runs twenty-one miles away from its lure—the distance spanning between a home where he is secure and a home where everything is now smeared with a suffocating haze the clouds fail to conceal.

"After you, Tim," Harvey tells him; he enters the room and drags his luggage along with him. Harvey closes the door behind him, locks it, and slides the key card into a small card slot affixed to the wall by the front door. Everything inside the room powers up all at once with a hiss—the air conditioning and the lights from the hallway, then to the kitchen, then to the ones above the two beds at the end of the room.

He begins unpacking his luggage. He hangs his two cotton button-down shirts (one is black and one is white) and two printed t-shirts on their respective hangers and secures his two black denim jeans and two cotton chino shorts on separate hangers with clips on the waist. He leaves his undies, together with other trip necessities, under his hanging clothes. After unpacking, he stands before the window the curtains drawn.

His godfather has passed, and he has brought along clothes that are unfit for the occasion.

Harvey quietly approaches him and stares in the direction where he is staring—the fence below, where there are two children strolling around with their parents accompanying them by the shore. Timothy looks upward and toward the horizon; it's already sunset, the sun a crisp sphere in the crimson skies, its shape shining on the line where it meets the calm waters. He doesn't say anything and sits on the bed closest to the windows.

A part of Timothy Salazar knows this will not end well. Another part of him compels him to leave. But first, he is needed tomorrow at his godfather's wake.

V

After his visit to his doctor three weeks ago, Timothy Salazar only eats twice every day, one in the morning and one in the evening. He skips lunch. His morning meal is the usual wheat bread partnered with bacon and egg, while his evening meal only consists of a plate of half-cup rice and ranch-style corned beef paired with two sunny side-up eggs. His excuse to his doctor is that he has been on a diet, which his doctor believes he stopped a year ago when he weighed a hundred and forty pounds. Now he weighs a hundred and twenty pounds.

As his body shrunk, he has lost the appetite to eat sometimes, making him detest what he sees in the mirror: his cheekbones have shrunk a little, revealing his hollow cheeks. His shoulders, once broad, have slightly narrowed. His lips have become chapped, relative to what remains unseen in his body, constructed once for the benefit of innocence but dismantled against its will by cracked skin.

You're home, Timothy. Now dive into me.

VI

In the afternoon, he is now drawn to one truth—that there is no obligation to attend his godfather's funeral. The name of his godfather alone is a funeral that he has no interest in attending, in expressing his sympathy, or in coming to terms with a grief that is nonexistent. When he stretches his arms out to the wind, a massive sense of liberty befalls upon him, a kind of sovereignty that releases him from an entity accountable for stripping him of a childhood he has failed to live.

He now stands still before the crushing waters, in conflict with staying and yearning for the jolt of the waves. He chooses what he yearns for, and it is calling him.

In a place like this, anywhere is not secure. Anywhere is an abstraction, with certainties turning into doubt, which turns into mistrust, which turns into fear. That sense of fear translates to melancholia burdened with the need to escape. Every moment steers him into different places, determining, with no warning, the source of his terrors. He gazes into the darkness and the stilled waters, and he desires to be one with them—an impaired self colliding with a body of water engulfed with contamination, a perfect clash of bodies parallel with each other. That is, he craves for its touch more than anyone else's, his mother's, his father's—even Harvey's, whose touch has created another home for him. No touch translates to comfort other than the water and the symphony of its waves. He walks closer to the water, his feet welcoming the sand's gritty hold on his skin, the water giving him an embrace that rewrites his understanding of what an embrace is. For him, an embrace has been a sign of comfort, but at this moment, an embrace with the waters equates with an exile from the place where he was born and a getaway from the burdens of existence, of breathing, of being human.

He feels his body twist, from his hips down to his legs and feet, causing him to collapse to the ground. From his feet, gray scales grow, expanding gradually through his feet and coating his skin. The pain, which he surprisingly finds pleasurable, pressures him to arch his back and squeeze his fingers. His feet and legs are now gone, covered with scales, raw fluke where his feet should be, and with anything beyond the ordinary and beyond what is possible. Continually, the scales grow and stretch upward, reaching his hips and creeping around his legs, replacing the flesh once disfigured by men who unjustly made use of his body against his will.

Slowly, Timothy Salazar has transfigured into the monster he once both dreamed of and feared becoming.

The waves and waters belong to you. The water is your body. Dive into me.

In his pure nakedness, accompanied by grace, he senses a familiar, rhythmic, graceful sway below him. With a smile he has never had in years, he dives into the water, the waves embracing the creature he has become, and once, deep in the water, in the endless darkness of possibilities beyond him, all he sees is light as he swims into what being free is—a crescendo of yielding to his point of becoming.

tsunami warning, facing shore⸻⸻⸻⸻⸻⸻

samudra:

     would-be glass-smasher,
mystic, crystallizing
rhythm to granular form on ripple-lakes.

     body an inner gravel.

on a landing stories-high,
so close to spray it nauseates volcanic,
     nothing between sumatra's face and roil.

i cannot look upwards—
though i know we mere insani, sandlocked,
have detected the waters
     lifting their fist.

     look at me who has always loved you
     and don't strike now.
     don't strike.

the truth is in remembering waves
that feel like blue-gray air
     about to turn,

     to make sea-cloud graves,
and vast sky cut from upturned basins,

heaven's lip, blooming purple into salt.

S E R I N A   R A H M A N

Fishermen Facing Down the Storms_____

Kami sebenarnya gadai nyawa demi dapatkan hasil laut untuk orang makan.
We are actually pawning our lives to catch seafood for people to eat.

—*Attan Tekok*

This was muttered to me as I sat at the Pasar Pendekar Laut (Sea Warriors Market) jetty, waiting for the fishermen to return with their catch. It was storming violently, and we were silently counting boats to make sure everyone had made it back. Some had managed to race to shore ahead of the menacing clouds. Those who were too far out when the winds suddenly changed direction were stuck. Some had tried to hide in the nearly nonexistent shelter of a parked container ship. Others waited for a break to face down the winds and waves that rose far higher than their twenty-foot-long boats to try to get home. Nowadays, they never know how bad the storms will get. These guys never forget their comrades, though. Several will tie themselves to border marker buoys to count heads—they always know who ventured out further than usual; they will wait for each other before making a break home. Then, at least, if anyone flips, there will be others there to help.

At the jetty, there is a quiet tension. The elders sit, eyes trained, at the entrance to our river. The younger ones in motorbike helmets and windbreakers go from boat to boat bailing out rainwater so that the boats and engines don't sink. These are basic fiberglass boats that don't drain themselves. There is no hiding from the elements in this trade. I pace back and forth on the jetty, doing what I can, ticking off names and noting the fish they send and their weights. I ask if they've seen the others and where they were when the storm hit.

One by one, they return, bedraggled and exhausted. Often with very little catch to show for the storm that they've just survived. It's often too dangerous for them to haul in their nets and lines. This is work they do standing up in the boat, which is just impossible in this crazy weather as they rock wildly in the surge with the waves washing onto their decks.

Money spent on petrol is burned with no returns. But they are just grateful to be back in one piece and hope that their nets and lines don't disappear. They head out again when the storm dies down to try to retrieve them. If they are lucky, there will be some sort of catch for them too. If they are more than unlucky, they won't be able to find their gear. It can cost them up to RM2500 to get a new set of lines or nets.

But you cannot put a price on your life.

...

This scenario was a frequent one over my 2.5 years helping out at the jetty during the Covid years. We are located at the western end of the Tebrau Strait between Singapore and Malaysia, in the southwestern corner of Johor. A string of fishing villages in the Tanjung Kupang subdistrict has been my home for the last fifteen years. I work in Singapore and commute daily across the Second Link Bridge, which is just five minutes to the right of our river estuary. As I sit in the inevitable immigration jam on the bridge going in to work every morning, I gaze down at our fishermen in the strait below and hope for their safe journey and a good catch in return for their toil.

I am a conservation scientist by training, and I study human-habitat interactions and uses of marine ecosystems, primarily in the Tebrau Strait, where we have vast seagrass meadows, coastal mangroves, and a tiny island rich with teeming intertidal rocky shores and soft coral reefs. The fishermen are my primary providers of information, as they are the true habitat experts of this area, spending every day reading the water, waves, currents, and weather to bring home the seafood and support their families. Over the Covid period, when our borders were closed and I couldn't head into Singapore to work, I parked myself at our jetty (where I previously could only help out on the weekends), and it allowed me to truly experience their world. In good weather and bad, they told me how the winds are and how the weather has changed over the years. They relate how the catch has moved or totally disappeared. I track their fish landings and collect data on species composition and changes. They also document, monitor, and report on endangered species that they encounter.

Our narrow strait, bound on both sides by industrial development, ports, and shipyards, is actually home to a multitude of charismatic creatures. Dugongs, two species each of turtles and crocodiles, four species of seahorses, countless pipefish and horseshoe crabs, and enigmatic rays such as the shovelnose, eagle, and bownose guitarfish ply our waters—all of which are endangered to some level. Our fishermen keep an eye on these species, and should an unfortunate specimen get caught on their lines or nets, they are released—but not before their photos are taken and an estimate of their weight and lengths is recorded. They then let me know where they saw it and its location. These habitat experts have helped us to map these species' locations, and they also know how and where they've moved over the years. This is the best of local ecological knowledge, a source of information that is incomparable to any other. No lab-based scientist has the depth and breadth of knowledge of a seaman who has seen these creatures in situ for years and has the added wisdom of his forefathers' understanding of their sea embedded in his soul.

I train local youth as citizen scientists and community researchers; they too gather natural heritage information from their elders and combine it with scientific structures as they conduct habitat mapping and other scientific research in our coastal ecosystems. This new holistic knowledge that they create brings together the best of both worlds and also incorporates local cultural heritage in relation to our natural areas and species. This information is then used in their community ecotourism efforts to help supplement local incomes, as well as in the environmental education that they conduct for other local or visiting youths. This pool of knowledge and input is also sought by developers and local agencies for myriad purposes, including habitat conservation.

…

Dulu, senang nak baca angin. Kalau angin barat – barat lah angin tu seminggu-dua. Sekarang, dalam sehari angin boleh tukar 3 ke 4 kali. Kita keluar angin selatan. Dah letak jaring tetiba angin naik tolak barat pulak. Tak sempat nak angkat jaring [dan] sembunyi.
In the past, it was easy to read the winds. If it was a westerly, it would stay that way for 1 or 2 weeks. Now, in one day it can change 3 or 4 times. We head out in southern winds. We put down our nets and suddenly the wind picks up and it becomes a westerly. We don't have time to pick up our nets and hide.
—*Abang Din Jambang*

The fishermen have deep wells of information. Chatting with them daily over the Covid period allowed me to hear torrid tales of the increasing difficulties they faced as they risked their lives at sea. I also saw how little catch they were bringing back as a result of these environmental changes. Over several months, the crab catch dwindled severely, and I witnessed fishermen coming home with just three or four crabs after several hours at sea. At other times, the prawn catch completely dried up, and there were no prawns to be found in waters that used to heave with myriad species of Penaeidae. In 2007, when I first arrived in these villages, crabs were coming up in the hundreds of kilos. In 2018, there were so many prawns caught that we struggled to find buyers for them. In 2020 and 2021, these species seemed to disappear.

A few fishermen told me that the crabs had moved. Some found them further inland and upriver—areas that are harder for them to head into because these are the hangouts of our estuarine crocodiles and false gharials. Others found them wandering further away from shore in much deeper waters. The fishermen put this down to changes in water temperatures, and this rang true—even the water at the jetty felt warmer to the touch.

Pasar Pendekar Laut imposes catch size restrictions for crabs; smaller crabs are released so that they have time to breed. "Empty" or "soft-shelled" crabs with less meat are also tossed back so that they have a chance to fill out and breed (mating often happens immediately after a female crab molts or changes its shell). But even these efforts have limited impact now. Increasingly frequent and far more ferocious storms have an effect on the catch. In the past, the calm after a storm usually promised a good crab haul. Over these two years, the storms sometimes seemed to melt into each other and barely pause, and the crabs seemed to bury themselves deep, refusing to emerge.

Warmer waters also mean more algae, and oftentimes the fishermen would come back looking even more exhausted as all they had were tons of offensive green muck that ruined their nets and required them to fork out more money to replace net fillings, yet barely produced any catch. Among the piles of green, they might perhaps only get one or two kilograms of acceptable-quality seafood, if at all. But aside from changes in species seasons and movements, the more severe storms simply meant that the fishermen couldn't head out to sea or had to abort their trips and return empty-handed. This resulted in a direct hit to their incomes. An inability to get out there means an inability to bring home the day's earnings.

...

Laut kami semakin kecil.
Our seas are getting smaller.
    —*Pak Long Karim*

The hurdles the fishermen face do not exist in silo. On top of the erratic weather and climate change impacts, there is also the relentless onslaught of coastal development and reclamation. All along this end of the Tebrau Strait, there are development projects that entail the creation of new islands for luxury resort homes, recreation and business enclaves, the extension of land, ports, and transshipment jetties, and even a huge petrochemical storage facility that will be meters away from a national park on what used to be the southernmost tip of continental Asia. I took a few fishermen to a new development that had come up over the past decade for them to see what it looked like from shore. They had only ever seen it from their boats.

As their wives swooned over the pretty fake beach and posed for photos at artificial Insta props, the men stood grimly on the beach with arms crossed. This new "land" they stood on used to be some of their most prolific crab and prawn holes. Several generations ago, their grandfathers had homes here, along the coast, with their fishing boats tied under their front porch, which hung conveniently over the water. In those days, they could just fish off their balconies, reeling in large groupers, snappers, and even more crustacea. There was so much bounty then that the fishermen had rules. Crabs with eggs were released. Only a certain amount of prawns could be caught at a time—they believed that a large spirit crocodile would follow their boats and do them harm if they didn't abide by these laws. Today, with the seas ever-shrinking, these rules have long been forgotten as fishermen battle for whatever they can bring home. When the prawns do appear, long-held taboos of maintaining calm countenance at sea are forsaken as they occasionally lose their cool and fight over fishing grounds and a space to put down their nets. When this happens, the prawns swiftly disappear, as the old tales predicted.

The ever-increasing scramble for limited resources is compounded by an increasing number of fishermen entering this space as fishing grounds die out with increased development and pollution along the strait. Fishermen from the eastern side wander ever further to bring home something, anything, encroaching on areas that are the unmarked and undeclared territories of other communities. But as none of these boundaries are formalized in verbal or written agreements, there is no stopping anyone from entering. Few keep to the traditional norms that used to preserve fish stock.

Even the Sustainable Fisheries Programme that Pasar Pendekar Laut imposes on its fishermen is sometimes hard to justify as there are many others who take home the species that our fishermen record and release. It is infuriating for them to see others make a quick buck from specimens that they didn't bring home—especially when there is little else in their nets. The local authorities are also in a bind as they have no legal jurisdiction to prevent the catch of these species as Malaysia did not ratify international agreements on their protection. They also have insufficient manpower to monitor the waters to boot. Our corner of the sea and the species that live within it seem to be in the stranglehold of both development and climate change. The noose is ever-tightening.

...

Kita tak boleh duduk menangis je. Barang laut semakin kurang. Nelayan sendiri terancam. Kita mesti cari jalan lain untuk dapat duit. Kami siapa je? Laut ni dah jadi hak orang lain.
We cannot just sit and cry. There is less catch. Fishermen are endangered. We must find a way to earn money. Who are we? The seas now belong to other people.

—*Shalan Jum'at*

Pasar Pendekar Laut was set up by Shalan Jum'at in 2016 to ensure that fishermen get a fair price for their catch. Today, the market pays the fishermen twice the amount they might earn elsewhere by decreasing the profit margin. The price for the consumer stayed the same for several years, until fish landings seemed to crash. With even less catch and rising costs of petrol and fishing equipment, prices had to increase a little bit to ensure that the fishermen can survive.

There are many obstacles in their way. As the wider economy struggles post-Covid and in the face of a looming global recession, many have lost their jobs and turned to fishing as a safety net. This means even more fishermen are squeezing into an already overcrowded space. Although development stopped over the Covid period, climate change impacts became increasingly visible. With one parameter on hold, it was clear that there was no other cause for the drop in catch. On top of that, fishermen are a marginalized community, with many among the bottom forty percent of society and the national income distribution scale. Decisions that have far-reaching impacts on the natural spaces that the fishermen depend on for a living are made in corridors of power far from the salty air and muddy substrates.

Yet another layer of problems these communities face is a lack of authentic representation. While there are purported fishing associations created to "speak for" and "assist" the community, many of these are politically motivated and less than transparent.

My time with the fishermen revealed that corruption, cronyism, and nepotism are the norm, and those who need the most help are often bypassed by those who have the right connections. While Pasar Pendekar Laut could improve local earnings and help widen the fishermen's market, there is little it can do to improve fish stocks or reduce the coastal development that adds to their woes.

What it has been able to do, however, is engage directly with the Fisheries Department, bypassing the local associations and village or fishermen's "heads" that often stand in their way. This has helped more of the local fishermen get fishing licenses, an asset that legalizes their effort and prevents them from being stopped by the marine police. It also gives them access to the many government assistance schemes on offer. This is exactly why these licenses are so highly sought after by those who rarely or never head out to sea. Thus, those who have the ability to control who can get those licenses ensure that they keep them among only friends and family.

Increased recognition of the fishermen and the market for their efforts toward sustainability and willingness to work together to help themselves (instead of just waiting for aid) have also garnered the attention of the media and local agencies. Initially afraid to speak to outsiders, the fishermen of Pasar Pendekar Laut are now more comfortable speaking in front of a camera when the media come by or to the many visitors who stop by the jetty to find out more. Customers who come for the high-quality fresh-off-the-boat catch are also taught about seafood seasonality and the need to pay a fair price. The fishermen themselves man and run the market and share their stories (and seafood recipes!) with the customers.

They now have a voice.

There is also a *warung* (foodstall) at the jetty with the fishermen's wives as chefs—not only to ensure that the fishermen have food and drinks when they return from sea, but to entice customers to buy up all the catch. Fish bought at the market can be immediately cooked here, and the scent of food cooking encourages everyone who wanders in to buy something so that they can eat there too.

...

No one knows how much longer fishing can be a viable livelihood or when the entire community might be displaced from even more development. But for now, the fishermen of Pasar Pendekar Laut in the Tanjung Kupang subdistrict are doing what they can to last for as long as they are allowed to. Too much is beyond their ken. But these sea warriors will do what they can to overcome the storm and survive.

My Mother Is a River

Mekong Delta, Việt Nam

nước nước nước
nước
nước
nước

is the sound of our survival

We are a country of water,
where thousands of rivers flow
like the arteries and veins in my body.

We are a people of water—
we plant and harvest rice,
ride our canoes and sampans,
walk knee deep in water, swim,
catch fish with our bare hands
and handmade nets.

We are a people who, at dawn,
ride our bamboo boats
out to gather morning dew
from lotus petals.

We walk barefoot through life,
our toes and legs dig into mud.

Mekong River delta soil,
water, imprinted into my DNA.

There are now cracks in the river
bottom with crevices
like the geography of a brain.
The delta is drying out where rice
once grew for thousands of years.

My mother once told me, "As long as
you have rice, you will survive."

What will villagers do now
with the numerous dams upstream?
Where will the fish go?
What is happening to the endangered
river dolphin, the giant catfish,
the softshell turtle?

Where would mặt trăng,
moon, see her own reflection?

ALVIN B. YAPAN

TRANSLATED BY BERNARD CAPINPIN

Flies in the Mountain of Water

Flies were feasting on the rafflesia's wilted flower when the group of vacationers hiking up Mount Isarog found it. Paeng didn't comprehend what was so special about the flower, although he was already told that it was the largest flower in the world. He would only recount to Milia, his wife, who was left at home, how he was bewildered by the forest. If only their son hadn't come, he wouldn't have joined. Until then, Paeng had yet to climb a mountain or enter a forest. Everything he saw around him struggled to survive. The trees were all flanked side by side, from the sapling up to the oldest tree. One could no longer determine where the branches and leaves of each one, shrouded by moss and vines, began or ended. The moss was boggy, even the soil that had been buried by inches of rotten leaves. The surroundings were damp from the occasional drizzle, which had turned to light rain, netting the leaves. Paeng couldn't believe that they had hiked for almost twelve hours and endured a winding trail through the wilderness not devoid of menacing leeches just for a flower, which, like a heap of kalabaw manure, was infested by flies. He thought that that was how black a wilted rafflesia was. When they approached it and the flies dispersed, Paeng saw that it had a taint of brown.

They saw the entire flower laid out. It had no leaves, and its width reached up to a meter. Paeng was surprised when the guide of Hagahag Mountaineers explained to them. The rafflesia is indeed large, but it is also the foulest-smelling flower in the whole world. It reminded him of the stench that woke him some days ago.

"We should find a fresh rafflesia. I didn't come here just to take a picture of a wilted flower swarming with flies," Mr. Guzman complained, as Paeng had expected. His companions only laughed, and Paeng joined laughing.

When the rafflesia was first discovered blossoming in the wilderness of the Isarog forest, the environmentalists were thrilled. The flower was now rarely seen, and the entire family was considered to be nearly extinct. They celebrated their wrong presumption and declared that the discovered flower added to Mount Isarog's national park status. Mr. Guzman hadn't visited then because, when the news erupted, the flower, which had bloomed for only six days, was by then wilting. So when he heard that another rafflesia had been found, he didn't hesitate to go. He put his work on hold, took an airplane bound for Bicol, and immediately scaled Mount Isarog. The one now in Isarog was said to be far more beautiful: the largest kind of rafflesia that was once seen on Mount Apo in 1882 and was more recently discovered in Antique only months ago.

Mr. Guzman was a writer from Manila. He was ten years younger than Paeng who was four years past forty. He wanted to be referred to as a writer more than a journalist. Although he wrote for the national paper, he only did it to pilfer material for the stories he writes. He only changed the names and tweaked the events a little; he gave the characters motives. He believed that working in the newspapers provided a goldmine of stories unmatched by the imagination of any writer. When he heard of the news of a rafflesia's discovery in Isarog, his interest was piqued because of the rumors of illegal logging in that place, supported by the politicians overseeing that area. For him, it was good to delve into this story's possibility. He might even aid in maintaining the sanctity of the protected areas of Isarog National Park. Mr. Guzman was the professor of Paeng's son, who accompanied him to ascend the mountain. One day, his son called him up to tell him that the writer would be staying with them. They also invited two more men to the guide's house so that there were many of them in case they encounter any danger. The rumors that Isarog was swarmed by the NPA hadn't subsided yet. They had all once been the writer's students, even the guide who was Peang's partner climbing the mountain. They carried the baggage and equipment in their large backpacks. Paeng and the writer were free to walk.

They took a photo of the wilting rafflesia after driving the flies away. The guide suggested they could document each stage of the rafflesia's life cycle. He was sure that there were some around the area because, according to the news, it wasn't the only one that had been found. It was somewhere around there, assured the guide to the writer whom the students knew to be writing a story about the rafflesia, so it was important that they find at least one. The writer hadn't mentioned it to them, but they didn't ask because he had said in class that he had a superstition to not talk about a story until it was written down.

It was already noon, and it was growing darker when they finished taking photos of the wilting rafflesia. Paeng was worried about the encroaching darkness. He knew that he would sleep beside his son in the tent, but he remained restless. Perhaps it was because he was the eldest in the group. Perhaps because they were all still strangers to the place, even though he could tolerate sleeping on the hard ground and he knew his companions were used to mountaineering. He felt the same when his son, Omeng, left to study in Manila. He was from that place, and whatever may befall them, he felt that he was responsible. That's why he joined them when the writer invited him to complete the group as they climbed to Isarog.

Each pair will have to walk a few meters apart from the other, said the guide. They will need to search the whole area for the rafflesia and scout for a place to set up their tent for the incoming night. It wasn't too hard to find a rafflesia. They only needed to be on the lookout for a particular vine. The guide taught them about the vine of a wild grape. The rafflesia's roots clung around a vine that had stalks with four elongated leaves each. A flower without leaves is a parasite. It took root within the vines, and when it grew, a large flower protruded out from its sheath, as if to seem that the vine itself was blooming.

If they had difficulty identifying the vine, they could follow the flies in the area or try to get a whiff of the rafflesia. In the cold forest of Isarog, its stench became more odious for flies. Paeng couldn't believe that even in the middle of the Isarog forest, flies could still be found.

* * *

After only a few days, flies had already infiltrated Paeng and Milia's home. They had been eating lunch. Mr. Guzman had just arrived with their son from Manila. They faced each other at a rectangular table. The writer was wearing a white kamisa and house shorts. They passed around Milia's chicken tinola. The writer was telling them how smart and diligent their only child was in class.

Mr. Guzman was relieved when Omeng raised his hand in class after he had asked who was from Bicol and could help him locate the rafflesia. He was worried that someone in his class who wasn't bright would raise his hand. He couldn't stand a few days without having someone sharp to talk to. As a writer, Mr. Guzman believed that meeting new people was good for his writing. So he relied on his current students to open up their homes to him as a guest. This way, he was made to talk about topics he didn't know he could talk about. He couldn't achieve that when he merely stayed at a hotel instead. He would only be surrounded by grinning waiters and guards. Nor could he have tasted Milia's delicious tinola, which Mr. Guzman praised.

He couldn't have experienced them all if he had stayed at the home of his previous student, who now guided them on their hike to Mount Isarog. It was good that his other two male students had also come to visit the home. They were already more than enough. They would probably talk about the story he had written about them. Those three students bravely joined the rallies at EDSA Tres. They pretended to be pro-Erap and pelted the police and anti-riot teams. When the three were asked in class about their experience, he asked them why they did it. Just for fun, they said. Just a whim. Mr. Guzman wrote a story about the three's experience. He made EDSA a game of hide and seek. If he had stayed at the guide's house, he would probably have been asked about what he wanted to depict in the story he wrote. He would probably be made to talk about his own life. He would be asked how he writes. He would be forced to list his superstitions and rituals one by one when writing. He would be interrogated on how he began writing, why he writes, and how much of what he wrote was based on his own life and experiences, or just from his imagination. He has already been to countless interviews and programs that have asked the same questions. Mr. Guzman told all of these to them and Paeng. He explained how he was pleased when Omeng raised his hand because, out of his many students, only he understood what he had discussed about the death of the author in class—how the life of the work was separate from the life of the author. Paeng felt that he couldn't be on par with Mr. Guzman's stature, though he only wore a simple top and house shorts.

At that moment, a fly was orbiting around the dining table. It first circled around and landed on the bowl of tinola. Paeng and Milia looked at each other. Milia drove the fly away. Paeng thought that it would be gone for good. But after a few moments, the fly returned and, to the embarrassment of the couple, landed on the writer's plate. Mr. Guzman suddenly drove it away with his hands, and it fled to who knows where.

Paeng could only bow his head. The writer knew that somewhere not far off was the family's pigpen. They sent Omeng to school in Manila with their earnings from this pigpen. They took all their earnings from the pigpen to improve it and make a shed for them. The couple hired two people to raise them because they had grown older and couldn't accomplish the heavy labor themselves. They already had regular pig buyers. Though the pigs had their own shed, it was still close enough to their house for the flies to come in from there. Paeng had already installed a screen in their house, but still, the flies came in. Paeng toured the writer around and showed him the pigpen. The metal pens adjacent to each other were cramped to round up the pigs and prevent them from growing too fast. Countless flies swarmed the area. Some landed on the pigs' white skins, and they appeared to be joining the piglets sucking their mother lying on the ground. The pigs were washed every day for them to remain clean and to prevent them from reeking. Mr. Guzman asked where they disposed of the pigs' excretions.

"There's a pit at the back," explained Paeng. "We dump the excrement there."

"It's good that there is no house nearby."

"That's how it is here. The houses are far apart."

The writer told them that they could make money out of the pigs's excrement. They could set up a biogas chamber. They could save on fuel. Paeng had once considered it. But when he asked around, he discovered that he needed a considerable sum of capital. He merely told the writer that they would probably set up the biogas after their son had finished college.

"Did you hear that, Bart?" joked the writer to their son, who could only muster a smile.

To Paeng's embarrassment at the flies entering their home, he told them a story. When Paeng was a boy, his parents made him believe that the flies entering the house at night were spirits. A relative who had died was visiting, so killing a fly was not good. Or even a small fly at night.

Mr. Guzman took an interest in Paeng's story. He laughed, and the couple's embarrassment subsided. Those who lived in the provinces were superstitious, which was nice to write a story about. He wanted to tell Paeng that in his class, a fly was a philosopher or a writer. He wanted Paeng to continue his story about the flies. But nothing followed. They were silent again. Mr. Guzman had to explain to them his purpose in going to Mount Isarog. Paeng and Milia had only then heard about the rafflesia. When Mr. Guzman mentioned that it was the largest flower in the world, they didn't understand the writer. Nor did they have a name for the flower. Even what they called stinking corpse here. The flower was said to have smelled like a corpse, so it was named. Even so, Paeng couldn't make anything of it, so he didn't understand until he saw the flower himself. The family of flowers was in danger of being extinct, as were the numerous birds, animals, and plants on Mount Isarog. Despite being declared a national park, some still ventured to cut down trees in Isarog.

Paeng only knew Isarog as the mountain he saw when he went out to the yard. Whenever he saw the waterfall of Isarog like a scratch on the mountain's face from their yard, it meant that the rain would be coming soon. The mountain couldn't seep all the water, so it released it to the wind as rain. Isarog was a mountain of water. If it should ever erupt once more, water would flow from its mouth and flood the towns scattered at its feet. It would shatter like an earthen jar filled with water once it erupts again.

Paeng had countlessly dreamt of Mount Isarog's eventual eruption, especially after Pinatubo's eruption in 1991, after six hundred eleven years of dormancy. In his dream, he knew that Isarog had already erupted, but he still couldn't wake up from his deep sleep. He would only wake up once his house had been swept away. He was the only one in the house; Milia and Omeng weren't to be found. The house would be completely flooded. The chairs and tables would float—even his own bed, the television and refrigerator, all their appliances. The walls and the columns of the house would topple to one side. The roof would crash. He would escape the house by swimming. He would encounter their dying pigs gasping and floating in the water. Paeng would see the whole barangay engulfed by the water spewed out by Isarog. He only saw the utility poles slightly jutting out above the water. Even the coconut treetop to which he clung, he hoped, would not be swept away by the current. He would wake up, praying for the waters not to rise further.

* * *

The guide partnered with Paeng as they searched for the rafflesia and a spot where they could pitch tents. He saw their other companions not far off. His son accompanied Mr. Guzman. He turned his gaze around the surrounding area. He saw nothing but ferns. Due to the sprawling vines dangling from the trees, he couldn't determine which one the rafflesia clung on to. He saw many orchids, like the ones sold in the market of his town, whenever those who lived at the foot of the mountain descended. They lingered by the sidewalks, watching over the orchids they had brought. They seldom went down. Oftentimes, it was only during the town's festival, the celebration of the feast of the Virgin of Peñafrancia, when the people scuffled in town like flies. Paeng's wife liked orchids, and he thought of picking one the next morning to give to Milia.

He and Milia had slept early the last night. Omeng and the writer were to leave early to trek to Isarog. The fragrance of the dama de noche wafted across the open window of their room. Though the breeze blew from the pigpen, its stench would be overcome by the dama de noche. It was good that he hadn't prevented Milia from growing the dama de noche. He had wanted her to cut it down because it had grown bushier and snakes might nest there. But he knew that Milia wouldn't listen, though he wanted the dama de noche cut, so he didn't bring it up. His wife liked to garden.

Milia's interest in gardening beside their house started when Omeng left to study in Manila. Because there was not much to do inside the house anymore, she took care of the garden. If Paeng was busy with the pigpen, the garden was Milia's domain. Milia had done numerous experiments just to make her orchids flower. She kept the orchid's roots inside eggshells. She watered them with her own urine. But the orchids wouldn't bloom. When they flowered, the flowers were small, and the colors were usually dull. Not like the orchids she saw in the yards of other houses. By then, she had learned that the orchids she had bought were different. The orchids she tended were introduced; that was why the flowers were not that large and their colors were dull. Milia had spent a lot to buy the best orchids. She had also bought chemicals to make them flower. The investment she made was not for nothing, and just after a few months, she saw the flowers of her vanda.

That was why Paeng hesitated to bring Milia orchids from the forest of Isarog. The flowers he saw were rather small compared to his wife's vanda. If size was mainly considered, there was the rafflesia's flower, though it was illegal to take it, and he wouldn't dare take it because of the smell. What Paeng didn't know was that the first orchid Milia grew was still there. She didn't throw it away because she grew fond of it, and even though its flowers were not as big as the vanda, thry were the most fragrant, especially the duck orchid that made the house's vicinity fragrant at night with the help of the dama de noche and the slender Chinese bamboo.

Before Omeng arrived with the writer, Milia spruced up the garden. She weeded out the grass, even the smallest green that protruded out of the soil. She was also the one who thought to prepare chicken tinola for

Mr. Guzman's first lunch with them. She didn't buy the chicken from the market. She slaughtered one of the hens wandering around the house. A chicken not raised in a cage had a different taste. It was sought after by those from Manila who went to the provinces. Milia heard from her friends who raised orchids, the friends she bought her plants from or gave plants to. She understood that the Manileños went to the provinces to escape from their city life and to refresh their zest for life. So they climbed mountains where there were few people and everything else was green. Milia's friends weren't wrong, and Mr. Guzman enjoyed the chicken tinola.

Milia also cleaned the whole house and asked Paeng to help arrange Omeng's room. The last time their son returned home was just after EDSA Dos. Though Omeng didn't mention it to them, they knew that he had joined it because they had religiously followed it on television when the pro-Erap group sieged the Malacañang. They laughed at how the rallyists had been able to grab hold of the truncheons and riot shields from the police and how they threw back the teargas thrown at them by the police. They needn't ask their son if he has joined EDSA Dos. If Rocco hadn't been a Bicolano, perhaps they would have voted for Erap. So they only watched it on television and witnessed all the events unfolding like a movie. They saw how a dead man had been left in front of the Malacañang. Nobody minded the man's corpse. It was left on the street while being surrounded by turmoil.

While Paeng and Milia slept after having cleaned the house, Paeng was woken up by the foul smell of decomposing material from inside the house. That morning, Paeng tried to search for the source of the smell. He flashed a light above the ceiling to check if a rat had died there. Many times, he had attempted to exterminate those families of rats, but the mother rat kept giving birth too much and too quickly that he couldn't locate where they could have burrowed. He also went out on the street to see if a cat had been hit and left to rot on the side of the road. But he didn't see any cats who had finished their nine lives. When Milia asked him what he was searching for and he told her of the foul smell, she told him that she didn't smell anything. She pointed at the pigpen toward Paeng. If he hasn't found a rat or cat, it might have come from the stench of their pigpen. Paeng had the pigpen cleaned that day, but the rotten stench hadn't gone from his nose. It had only disappeared when he smelled the fragrance of the dama de noche when the wind blew through the open window and into their room.

* * *

Fireflies were already appearing, and the surrounding noise was changing, but they still hadn't located the rafflesia. The guide, who was Paeng's partner, had already decided where they would set up the tent when they heard screaming. The screaming had a stroke of fear, but it was obvious that it was trying to keep itself from panicking. The screams came from the two male students. As they heard the screams, Mr. Guzman and Omeng joined the guide and Paeng.

"There's a body," said one, while the second pointed his finger to the area.

The writer was delighted. At last, a rafflesia had been found. His excursion to Isarog would not be put to waste. But the two students shook their heads. When two accompanied them to the area they had pointed to, they saw a woman's body. The corpse was feasted on by flies. Ants were crawling toward it. She wore jeans in the mud. Her t-shirt was soaked to her body because of the damp surroundings. Her eyes, wide open, were pale. The body was already stiff, they presumed. Perhaps if they had moved the body, they would have seen worms. They couldn't figure out how many hours or days it had been here. The two students had followed the stench of the body. They mistook it for rafflesia; they were shocked to have found a body in the middle of the forest.

They all looked at each other. The two men who had first seen the body were scared stiff. Until the slow and certain drops of rain in the area came, their heads and bodies were drenched by the image of the woman's corpse lying exposed before them. It seared into their minds. Then they felt how their fear and unease were being cultivated. First, fear: a sapling of apitong sprang out and grew in bewilderment skyward, became a monument in the middle of the forest, stretched out its branches, and sprouted leaves. They jumped out of their skins. It was then that they were plagued by doubt and worry, vines that constricted their bodies. What if the woman's killer was still around? What if they were accused of being the killers? How will they prove their innocence? What if the corpse wasn't supposed to be found? They would certainly be on the news. They would read their names in the papers. They would be known as the group that had killed the woman. Their fear grew even larger and wider until the leaves fell in layers to the ground to calm them. The leaves softened the ground they stood on. That's why the fruits that fell from the trees that continued to grow didn't make a sound. They needed to calm down. They were adults. All of them are men. Whatever happens will happen.

"We need to notify the park ranger immediately," advised Omeng.

"We need to go down and inform the police," agreed one of the two men who found the body.

"I don't know the way through the dark. We might get lost," confessed the guide.

They all looked at the guide. They couldn't believe what he had told them. They couldn't stand to think of sleeping here with a corpse lying just a few meters away from them. The guide felt that his fear was suddenly infested with termites. Anthills on the ground have swelled and burst like a volcano. The termites have scattered. Some have taken wing to assail the guide's fear of being lost in the dark. But nothing could match the durability and strength of the apitong. It couldn't be easily toppled by termites. The guide could do nothing but bow in shame.

They merely listened to Mr. Guzman, even though he believed in a superstition not to talk about his story until it was written down. He didn't stop talking, and they couldn't do anything else but listen. He would write that perhaps the woman had been a member of the NPA and a comrade or the military had informed her. But the story would be better if she was found out to be one of the residents protecting Mount Isarog. She might have discovered ties between the DENR and some illegal loggers, so she was slain and dumped in the mountains to be mistaken for an NPA member. Mr. Guzman spoke of endless possibilities for his story. Paeng only felt that Omeng was by his side. He felt that he was again inside the nightmare where Mount Isarog erupted. He felt as if he was drowning again. But now he was not in the water, but among all the things he saw in the forest, he struggled to survive. Then the flowers emerged around him. They burst into color, from the blackest to the most colorful rainbows. The fragrances mixed from the wildest to the foulest odors. Moss enveloped everything, from the young seedling to the rotting corpse. They gave deference to the fear contained in each one. With their abashed eyes, they shifted their gaze around them. Until they were no different from the trees of the forest. They were deeply rooted in the ground they stood on. They remained stationary like living idols in the middle of the forest.

Again, Paeng smelled the rafflesia feasted on by flies. He remembered how Mr. Guzman declared that the author was dead; the author had been dead the day the flies had entered their home, which Paeng, after descending Mount Isarog, would later recount to his wife, crying and wrapped around his wife's chest, saying how he was bewildered by the forest's savagery.

Translation by Bernard Capinpin.

Mga Bangaw sa Bundok ng Tubig———————————

PINAGPIPISTAHAN ng mga bangaw ang lanta nang bulaklak ng rafflesia, nang datnan ng pangkat ng mga bakasyunistang umakyat sa Bundok ng Isarog. Hindi maintindihan ni Paeng kung ano ang espesyal sa bulaklak, kahit sinabi na sa kanyang ito ang pinakamalaking bulaklak sa buong mundo. Ikukuwento na lamang niya kay Milia, ang asawa niyang naiwan sa bahay, kung paano hindi niya maintindihan pati ang kagubatan. Kung hindi nga lang kasama ang anak nila, hindi na sana siya sumama. Noon lamang talaga nakaakyat ng bundok si Paeng at nakapasok ng gubat. Nagpapaligsahang mabuhay ang lahat ng makita niya sa paligid. Magkakaagapay ang mga puno mula sa papausbong pa lamang hanggang sa pinakamatanda. Hindi na matiyak kung saan nagtatapos at nagsisimula ang sanga at dahon ng bawat isang nadadamtan ng lumot at baging. Malambot sa lumot pati ang lupa na natatabunan ng ilang pulgada ring magkakapatong na dahong nabubulok. Basang-basa ang paligid sa panaka-nakang ambon na nagiging payapang tikatik ng ulang nalalambat ng mga dahon. Hindi matanggap ni Paeng na umakyat sila nang halos labindalawang oras at sumuong sa pasikut-sikot na daan sa kasukalang hindi na nawalan ng banta ng mga limatik para lamang sa isang bulaklak na nilalangaw at parang bunton ng tae ng kalabaw. Akala niya ganoon nga kaitim ang lantang rafflesia. Nang lapitan nila at mabulabog ang mga bangaw, nakita ni Paeng na may bahid ito ng kayumanggi.

Buong bulaklak ng rafflesia ang nakita nilang bunton. Wala itong dahon at umaabot nang halos isang diyametro ang lapad. Nabigla si Paeng nang ipaliwanag sa kanila ng giyang kasapi ng Hagahag Mountaineers. Higante nga ang rafflesia ngunit isa rin ito sa pinakamabahong bulaklak sa buong mundo. Ipinaalala sa kanya nito ang nabubulok na amoy na gumising sa kanya, mga ilang araw pa lamang ang nakakalipas.

"Kaya dapat makakita tayo ng sariwa pang rafflesia. Hindi ako pumunta dito para lamang kunan ng litrato ang bulaklak na lanta at nilalangaw." Tulad ng inaasahan ni Paeng, nagreklamo si Mr. Guzman. Nagtawanan na lamang ang mga kasama niya, at nakitawa na rin si Paeng sa kanila.

Nang unang matuklasan ang nakabukadkad na mga talulot ng rafflesia sa kasukalan ng gubat ng Isarog, nagkagulo ang mga environmentalist. Bihira

nang makita ang bulaklak at pinangangambahang lipol na ang buong pamilya. Ipinagdiwang nila ang kanilang mga maling haka-haka at idineklara ang
natuklasang bulaklak bilang karagdagang yaman ng pagiging national park
ng Bundok ng Isarog. Hindi nakabisita si Mr. Guzman noon dahil nang
lumabas sa diyaryo ang balita, papalanta na ang bulaklak na umaabot
lamang nang anim na araw ang pamumukadkad. Kaya nang marinig niyang
may nakita muling rafflesia, hindi na siya nag-atubiling pumunta. Inihinto
niya ang lahat ng kanyang trabaho, sumakay ng eroplano papuntang Bikol
at dali-daling inakyat ang Bundok ng Isarog. Higit na maganda raw ang
nakita ngayon sa Isarog: ang pinakamalaking klase ng rafflesia na minsan
lamang natagpuan sa Bundok ng Apo noong 1882, at kakatuklas pa lamang
nang ilang buwan sa Antique.

Isang manunulat si Mr. Guzman galing Maynila. May sampung gulang
lamang ang bata niya kay Paeng na apat na taon na ring nakatapak ang edad
sa kuwarenta. Higit na nais niyang tawaging manunulat kaysa sa mamama-
hayag. Nagsusulat man siya para sa mga pambansang pahayagan, ginagawa
lamang niya ito upang magkaroon ng materyal para sa mga isusulat na
kuwento. Pinapalitan na lamang niya ang mga pangalan at binabago nang
kaunti ang mga pangyayari; binibigyan ng motibo ang mga tauhan.
Naniniwala siyang kabang-yaman ang pagtatrabaho sa pahayagan ng
mga kuwentong hindi mapapantayan ng imahinasyon ng sinumang manunulat. Nang marinig niya halimbawa ang pagkakatuklas ng rafflesia sa
Isarog, nahuli ang interes niya dahil sa mga kuwento ng ilegal na patotroso
sa lugar na sinusuportahan din ng mga politikong nanunungkulan sa pama-
halaan. Magandang saliksikin para sa kanya ang posibilidad ng kuwentong
ito. Maaari pa siyang makatulong sa pagpapanatiling sagrado ng kinakaling-
gang mundo ng national park sa Isarog. Propesor si Mr. Guzman ng anak
na lalaki ni Paeng, na kapareha nito sa pag-akyat ng bundok. Isang araw,
tumawag na lamang kay Paeng ang anak niya upang ipagpaalam na maki-
kituloy sa kanila ang manunulat. Nagsama din sila ng dalawa pang lalaking
nakitira sa bahay ng giya, nang marami sila pag-akyat ng Isarog, sakali mang
makaharap nila ang anumang panganib. Hindi pa rin namamatay ang mga
bali-balitang pinamumugaran ng mga NPA ang Isarog. Naging estudyante
silang lahat ng manunulat pati ang giya na kapareha ni Paeng sa pag-akyat
ng bundok. Sila ang may dala ng lahat ng balutan at kasangkapan sa nagla-
lakihan nilang backpack. Malayang nakapaglalakad sina Paeng at ang
manunulat.

Kinunan na rin nila ng litrato ang lantang rafflesia pagkatapos bugawin
ang mga bangaw. Mungkahi ng giya, maaari nilang idokumento ang bawat
yugto ng buhay ng rafflesia. Nakasisiguro siyang may iba pa sa paligid dahil
hindi lang naman daw isa ang nakita ayon sa balita. Naroon lamang sa lugar
na iyon, pagtitiyak ng giya sa manunulat na alam ng mga estudyanteng may
isusulat na kuwento tungkol sa rafflesia kaya't mahalagang makakita sila ng
kahit man lamang isa. Hindi man binabanggit sa kanila ng manunulat, hindi

na nila itinatanong dahil sinabi nito sa klaseng may pamahiin siyang huwag pag-usapan ang kuwento hangga't hindi pa naisusulat.

Hapon at papadilim na nang matapos nilang kunan ng litrato ang lantang rafflesia. Nag-alala si Paeng sa paparating na dilim. Alam man niyang matutulog siya katabi ng kanyang anak sa loob ng tent, hindi pa rin siya mapakali. Marahil dahil siya ang pinakamatanda sa pangkat. Marahil dahil kahit hindi naman niya mamasamain ang matulog sa matigas na lupa at kahit alam niyang sanay ang mga kasama niya sa mountaineering, dayo pa rin silang lahat sa lugar. Naramdaman niya ito, pati sa kanyang anak na si Omeng nang mag-aral na ito sa Maynila. Siya ang taga-roon at anumang mangyari sa kanila, nararamdaman niyang siya ang responsable. Kaya sumama siya nang imbitahan ng manunulat na kumpletuhin ang pangkat na aakyat sa Isarog.

Maglalakad sila nang magkakalayo nang ilang dipa ang bawat pareha, sabi ng giya. Sasaliksikan nila ang buong paligid para sa bulaklak ng rafflesia at para na rin sa paghahanap ng lugar na mapagtutulusan ng kanilang mga tutulugang tent para sa paparating na gabi. Hindi naman daw mahirap hanapin ang rafflesia. Babantayan lang nila ang isang partikular na baging. Itinuro sa kanila ng giya ang baging ng ligaw na ubas. May apat na pahabang dahon ang bawat tangkay ng baging na pinagkakapitan ng mga ugat ng rafflesia. Parasito ang bulaklak na walang dahon. Nagkakaugat ito sa loob ng baging at kapag matanda na, nagpapausli ng higanteng bulaklak sa mismong balat nito kung kaya aakalaing ang baging ang namumulaklak.

Kung mahirapan man silang kilalanin ang baging, maaari naman daw nilang sundan ang mga bangaw sa paligid o kaya ang amoy ng rafflesia. Sa lamig ng gubat ng Isarog, lalong tumitingkad ang baho nito para sa mga bangaw. Hindi makapaniwala si Paeng na kahit sa gitna ng kagubatan ng Isarog, may matatagpuan pa ring mga bangaw.

* * *

NANG NAKALIPAS na araw lamang, may nakapasok na bangaw sa kabahayan nina Paeng at Milia. Kumakain sila noon ng hapunan. Kadarating pa lamang ni Mr. Guzman at ng anak nila galing sa Maynila. Magkakaharap sila sa parihabang hapag. Nakasuot lamang ang manunulat ng puting kamisadentro at pambahay na shorts. Pinagsasaluhan nila ang nilutong tinolang manok ni Milia. Ikinukuwento noon ng manunulat kung gaano katalino at kasipag sa loob ng klase ang kaisa-isa nilang anak.

Nakahinga raw nang maluwag si Mr. Guzman nang magtaas ng kamay si Omeng sa klase, pagkatapos niyang magtanong kung sino ang taga-Bikol sa kanila at maaaring tumulong sa kanya sa paghahanap ng rafflesia. Natakot siyang baka ang magtaas ng kamay ay hindi gaanong magaling sa klase. Hindi niya matatagalan ang ilang araw nang walang matinong makakausap. Bilang manunulat, naniniwala si Mr. Guzman na maganda para sa pagsusulat niya na makisalamuha siya parati sa mga hindi niya kakilala. Kaya nagtawag na lamang siya ng kasalukuyan niyang estudyante na puwedeng pagbuksan ang tahanan sa kanya bilang bisita. Sa ganitong paraan, mapipilitan siyang makipagtalakayan tungkol sa mga paksang hindi niya alam na puwede pala niyang pag-usapan. Hindi niya iyon magagawa kapag tumuloy siya sa hotel. Paliligiran lamang siya ng mga nakangiting waiter at guwardiya. Ni hindi siya makakatikim ng ganoon kasarap na tinola, pagpupuri ni Mr. Guzman sa luto ni Milia.

Hindi rin niya ito mararanasan kung makikitulog naman siya sa bahay ng dati niyang estudyante na magiging giya nila sa pag-akyat ng Isarog. Tama nang ang dalawa pa niyang naging estudyanteng lalaki ang maging bisita nito sa bahay. Masyado na silang marami doon. Hindi malayong ang pag-uusapan lamang nila ay ang isinulat niyang kuwento tungkol sa kanila. Nangahas ang tatlong estudyante niyang ito na makisali sa mga rallyista ng EDSA Tres. Nagpanggap silang mga pro-Erap at nakibato rin ng mga pulis at anti-riot teams. Nang ikuwento ng tatlo sa klase ang naging karanasan nila, tinanong niya kung bakit nila ginawa iyon. Katuwaan lamang daw. Trip lang. Ginawan ng kuwento ni Mr. Guzman ang salaysay ng tatlo. Ginawa niyang laro ng taguan at habulan ang EDSA. Kung doon siya makikitulog sa bahay ng giya, hindi malayong tatanungin siya kung ano ba talaga ang nais niyang ipahiwatig sa isinulat niyang kuwento. Hindi rin malayong pagkuwentuhin siya tungkol sa sarili niyang buhay. Tatanungin siya kung paano siya nagsusulat. Mapipilitan siyang isa-isahin na naman ang mga pamahiin niya't ritwal sa pagsusulat. Uusisain kung paano siya nagsimulang magsulat, kung bakit siya nagsusulat, kung ilang porsiyento ba ng mga isinusulat niya ang halaw sa sarili niyang buhay at karanasan o likhang-isip lamang ba ang lahat. Ilang panayam na rin at palatuntunan ang dinaluhan niyang tinatanong ang mga parehong katanungan. Ikinuwento ang lahat ng ito ni Mr. Guzman kina Paeng. Ipinaliwanag niya ang tuwang naramdaman niya nang magtaas ng kamay si Omeng dahil siya lamang sa napakaraming estudyante ang nakaintindi nang sabihin niya sa harap ng klase na patay na ang may-akda, na may sariling buhay ang akda na hiwalay sa buhay ng manunulat. Pakiramdam ni Paeng hindi niya makakausap si Mr. Guzman, kahit pa nakaputing pantaas lamang ito at nakapambahay na shorts.

Noon nagsimulang umali-aligid ang bangaw sa hapag-kainan. Nagpaikut-ikot na muna ito saka dumapo sa labi ng mangkok ng tinola. Nagkatinginan sina Paeng at Milia. Binugaw ni Milia ang bangaw. Akala ni Paeng aalis na ito nang tuluyan. Ngunit makalipas lamang ang ilang sandali, muling bumalik ang bangaw at, sa hiya ng mag-asawa, umapak sa pinggan ng manunulat. Agad itong binugaw ni Mr. Guzman ng kamay niya at lumipad kung saan.

Napayuko na lamang si Paeng. Alam ng manunulat na sa di-kalayuan ng bahay nila, matatagpuan ang kabuhayang babuyan ng pamilya nila. Ang kita nila sa babuyang ito ang nagpaaral kay Omeng sa Maynila. Kinukuha nila ang lahat ng gastusin sa babuyang pinalakihan nila kinalaunan at pinagawan ng sariling bahay. Nangupahan ang mag-asawa ng dalawang tao na man-gangalaga rito dahil tumatanda na rin sila at hindi na kaya ang mabibigat na trabaho. May regular na rin silang tagabili ng baboy. Ngunit may sarili mang bahay ang babuyan, malapit pa rin ito sa kabahayan nila upang doon manggaling ang bangaw. Pinalagyan na ni Paeng ng screen ang bahay nila pero ano't nakapasok pa rin ang bangaw. Inikot at ipinakita pa ni Paeng sa manunulat ang babuyan. Maliliit ang magkakatabing de-bakal na kural nang huwag gaanong maging malikot ang mga baboy at mabilis tumaba. Maraming bangaw sa paligid. Nakadapo sa mapuputing balat ng mga baboy at nakikisalo sa mga biik na sumususo sa inahing nakalupasay sa sahig. Pinaliliguan nang araw-araw ang mga baboy nang huwag bumaho at man-atiling malinis. Itinanong ni Mr. Guzman kung saan nila dinadala ang mga dumi ng baboy.

"May hukay po sa likod," paliwanag ni Paeng. "Doon namin tinatambak ang mga tae."

"Buti ho wala kayong kalapit na bahay."

"Gano'n po talaga dito. Magkakalayo ang mga bahay."

Sinabi ng manunulat na maaari raw nilang pagkakitaan ang dumi ng baboy. Maaari silang magpatayo ng bio-gas. Makakatipid sila sa gagamitin nilang panggatong. Naisipan na ito minsan ni Paeng. Ngunit nang magta-nung-tanong siya, natuklasan niyang malaki-laki rin ang puhunan na kakai-langanin niya. Sinabi na lamang niya sa manunulat na marahil magtatayo sila ng bio-gas kapag tapos na ang anak nila sa kolehiyo.

"Narinig mo ba iyon, Bart?," biro ng manunulat sa anak nilang lalaki na napangiti na lamang.

Sa hiya ni Paeng sa nakapasok na bangaw sa kabahayan, nagkuwento na lamang siya. Nang bata pa si Paeng, pinaniwala siya ng mga magulang niyang kaluluwa ang mga bangaw na nakakapasok sa kabahayan sa gabi. Mga bumibisita itong kaluluwa ng mga namatay nilang ninuno kaya masa-mang pumatay ng bangaw. o kahit man lang langaw, sa gabi.

Natuwa naman si Mr. Guzman sa kuwento ni Paeng. Tumawa siya at naibsan ang hiya ng mag-asawa. Puno ng pamahiin ang mga taga-probin-siya na magaganda ring gawan ng kuwento. Nais sana niyang sabihin kay Paeng na sa loob ng klase niya ang bangaw ay isang pilosopo o manunulat. Gusto sana niyang ipagpatuloy ni Paeng ang kuwento nito tungkol sa ban-gaw. Ngunit wala na itong isinunod. Muli silang natahimik. Napilitan si Mr. Guzman na ipaliwanag sa kanila ang pakay niya sa Bundok ng Isarog. Noon lamang narinig nina Paeng at Milia ang rafflesia. Nang sabihin ni Mr. Guzman na ito ang pinakamalaking bulaklak sa buong mundo, hindi nila naintindihan ang manunulat. Ni wala silang alam na pangalan para sa bulaklak. Kahit ang tawag ditong bunga-bangkay. Amoy bangkay raw kasi ang bulaklak kaya tinawag nang ganoon. Pati ito'y hindi lubos mawari ni Paeng kaya hindi niya naintindihan hanggang sa makita niya mismo ang halaman. Nanganganib nang mamatay ang pamilya ng halamang ito at ang napakarami pang ibon, hayop, at halaman sa Bundok ng Isarog. Idineklara nang national park, may mga nangangahas pa ring pumutol ng puno sa Isarog.

Kilala lamang ni Paeng ang Isarog bilang bundok na natatanaw niya paglabas sa bakuran. Kapag nakikita mula sa bakuran nila ang talon ng Isarog na parang kalmot sa mukha ng bundok, nangangahulugan itong paparating na ang ulan. Hindi na makayang simsimin ng bundok ang lahat ng tubig kaya pinakakawalan na lamang sa hangin bilang ulan. Bundok ng tubig ang Isarog. Kapag muli raw pumutok, tubig ang lalabas sa bunganga nitong lulunod sa mga bayang nagkalat sa paanan. Parang tapayang puno ng tubig daw itong mababasag kapag muling sumabog.

Ilang ulit na ring napanaginipan ni Paeng ang muling pagsabog ng Bundok ng Isarog, lalo na nang muling pumutok ang Bulkang Pinatubo noong 1991 pagkatapos ng anim na daan at labing-isang taong pananahimik. Sa panaginip niya, alam na niyang sumabog na ang Isarog, hindi pa rin siya magising sa malalim na pagtulog. Magigising na lamang siya kapag inaanod na ang bahay nila. Siya lamang mag-isa sa bahay; wala sina Milia at Omeng. Babahain ang buong kabahayan. Lulutang ang mga upuan at mesa, pati ang kanyang higaan, ang telebisyon at ref, ang mga appliances. Gigiray pakaliwa ang mga dingding at poste ng bahay. Babagsak ang bubong. Lalabas siya ng bahay nang lumalangoy. Makakasalubong niya ang mga naghihingalo at sumisinghap nilang baboy na lumulutang-lutang sa tubig. Makikita ni Paeng ang buong barangay nilang nilamon na ng tubig na iniluwa ng Isarog. Ang mga poste na lamang ng kuryente ang nakikita niyang nakausli sa tubig. Pati ang ilang ulo ng puno ng niyog kung saan siya kakapit nang huwag ianod ng agos. Magigising na lamang siyang nagdarasal na sana huwag nang tumaas pa ang tubig.

* * *

Kapareha ni Paeng ang giya sa paghahanap ng rafflesia at pagtutulusan nila ng tent. Nakikita niya sa di-kalayuan ang iba pa nilang kasamahan. Kasama ng anak niya si Mr. Guzman. Iginala ni Paeng ang paningin niya sa paligid. Wala siyang makita kundi mga puno ng pakô. Sa dami ng baging na naglambitin sa mga puno, hindi niya makilala kung alin sa mga ito ang pinagkakapitan ng rafflesia. Maraming orkidya siyang nakita, katulad ng mga ibinebenta sa palengke sa bayan kapag bumababa ang mga nakatira sa paanan ng bundok. Nandoon sila, binabantayan sa bangketa ang ibinaba nilang mga orkidya. Minsan lamang sila kung bumaba. Kadalasan kapag may kasiyahan sa bayan, kapag ipinagdiriwang ang kapistahan ng Birhen ng Peñafrancia, kung kailan parang langaw sa dami ang mga taong dumudumog sa kabayanan. Mahilig sa orkidya ang asawa ni Paeng at naisipan niyang kumuha ng isa kinaumagahan upang dalhin kay Milia.

Maaga silang natulog ni Milia nang nakalipas na gabi. Maaga silang aalis ni Omeng at ng manunulat sa pag-akyat ng Isarog. Mula sa nakabukas na bintana ng kuwarto nila ni Milia, pumapasok ang samyo ng dama de noche. Nagpasalamat si Paeng at maraming itinanim na dama de noche ang asawa niya sa paligid ng bahay. Umihip man ang hangin mula sa babuyan, matatabunan ang baho nito ng dama de noche. Buti na lamang at hindi niya pinigilan si Milia sa pagpapalago ng dama de noche. Balak pa naman sana niyang ipaputol ito dahil kumakapal na't baka pamugaran ng mga ahas. Ngunit marahil alam na rin niyang hindi rin siya pakikinggan ni Milia, ipa-putol man niya ang dama de noche kaya hindi na niya ito pinagsabihan. Mahilig mag-alaga ng tanim ang asawa niya.

Nagsimula ang hilig ni Milia sa pagpapaganda ng halamanan sa paligid ng bahay nang umalis na si Omeng upang mag-aral sa Maynila. Dahil wala nang ibang pagkakaabalahan sa loob ng bahay, inatupag na lamang niya ang hardin. Kung ang babuyan ang pinagkakaabalahan ni Paeng, ang hardin naman ang naging lugar ni Milia. Lahat ng pagpapasya sa hardin ay gina-gawa lahat ni Milia. Marami ring pinagdaanang eksperimento si Milia mapabulaklak lamang ang mga orkidya. Nandoong balutin niya ng balat ng itlog ang ugat ng mga orkidya. Nandoong diligin niya ng kanyang ihi. Ngunit hindi pa rin mamulaklak ang mga orkidya. Kung mamulaklak man, maliliit ang mga bulaklak at kadalasa'y hindi matitingkad ang kulay. Hindi katulad ng nakikita niyang mga orkidya sa bakuran ng ibang tahanan. Noon niya natuklasang ibang uri pala kasi ng orkidya ang nabili niya. Mga ligaw na orkidya ang kanyang mga inaalagaan, kaya hindi gaanong malalaki ang bulaklak at hindi matingkad ang kulay. Gumastos din nang malaki si Milia, makabili lamang ng magandang klase ng orkidya. Bumili na rin siya ng gamot na pampabulaklak. Hindi naman napunta sa wala ang puhunang inilabas niya at makatapos lamang ng ilang buwan, nakakita na siya ng bulaklak ng vanda.

Kung kaya nagdalawang-isip si Paeng kung dadalhan pa ba niya si Milia ng orkidya galing sa gubat ng Isarog. Ang mga bulaklak na nakikita niya ay pawang maliliit kung ihahambing sa vanda ng asawa niya. Kung palakihin naman ng bulaklak, nandiyan sana ang bulaklak ng rafflesia, bawal nga lang pitasin, at hindi niya pagtatangkaang pitasin dahil sa baho. Hindi lamang alam ni Paeng, nandoon pa rin ang mga unang inalagaang orkidya ni Milia. Hindi na niya nakuhang itapon dahil napamahal na siguro sa kanya at kahit maliliit ang bulaklak nito at hindi kasinlaki ng vanda, ito naman ang pinakamababango, lalung-lalo na ang hugis-kalapating orkidya na nagpapa-bango sa paligid ng bahay tuwing gabi katulong ng mga bulaklak ng dama de noche at ng balingkinitang kawayang Tsino.

Bago pa man dumating si Omeng kasama ang manunulat, pinaganda ni Milia ang hardin. Binunot ang mga damo hanggang sa pinakamaliliit na luntiang umuusli pa lamang sa lupa. Siya rin ang nagbalak na maghanda ng tinolang manok para sa unang hapunan ni Mr. Guzman sa kanila.

Hindi siya bumili ng manok sa palengke. Ang isa sa mga inahing manok na pagala-gala lamang sa paligid ang kinatay niya. Iba ang lasa ng manok na hindi pinataba sa loob ng kulungan. Hanap-hanap daw ito ng mga taga-Maynila kapag bumibisita sa probinsiya, narinig ni Milia sa mga naging kaibigan niya sa pangangalaga ng orkidya, mga kaibigang napagbilhan o binilhan niya ng mga halaman. Kailangan daw niyang maintindihang pumupunta sa probinsiya ang mga Manileño upang makapagpahinga sa kanilang buhay-lungsod at muling mapanariwa ang sigla nila sa buhay. Kaya, umaakyat ang mga ito sa bundok kung saan wala gaanong tao at lahat ay luntian. Hindi nga nagkamali ang mga kaibigan ni Milia at nagustuhan ni Mr. Guzman ang tinolang manok.

Nilinis din ni Milia ang buong bahay at pinatulong si Paeng sa pag-aayos ng kuwarto ni Omeng. Huling umuwi ang anak nila pagkatapos lamang ng EDSA Dos. Hindi man ikuwento sa kanila ni Omeng, alam nilang sumali ito dahil sa masugid na pagsubaybay nito sa telebisyon nang sumugod ang mga pro-Erap sa Malakanyang. Pinagtawanan nito kung paano naaagawan ng mga rallyista ng mga batuta at panangga ang mga pulis, kung paano nila muling ibinabato pabalik sa mga pulis ang ibinato sa kanilang teargas. Hindi na tinanong nina Paeng ang anak nila kung sumali nga ba ito sa EDSA Dos. Kung hindi lamang Bikolano si Rocco, hindi malayong si Erap na rin sana ang ibinoto nila. Kaya nanood na lamang sila ng telebisyon at tiningnan ang lahat ng mga pangyayari na parang pelikula. Nakita nila kung paano may naiwang napatay na lalaki sa harap ng gate ng Malakanyang. Walang pumapansin sa bangkay ng lalaki. Nakahandusay lamang ito sa kalsada habang nagkakagulo ang lahat sa paligid.

Nang natutulog na sina Paeng at Milia kinagabihan ng kanilang paglilinis ng bahay, nagising na lamang si Paeng sa baho ng nabubulok na bagay sa loob ng kabahayan. Hinanap ni Paeng kinaumagahan kung saan nanggagaling ang amoy na iyon. Inilawan niya ang kisame dahil baka may dagang namatay doon. Ilang ulit na niyang sinikap lipulin ang pamilya ng dagang iyon ngunit sadyang napakarami at napakabilis manganak ng inahing daga na hindi niya matunton kung saang lungga nagtatago. Lumabas din siya ng kalsada upang tingnan kung may pusang nasagasaan at nabubulok sa tabi ng daan. Ngunit wala naman siyang nakitang pusang naubusan ng siyam nitong buhay. Nang tanungin siya ni Milia kung ano ang hinahanap niya at sabihin niyang may mabaho, wala naman daw itong naaamoy. Itinuro na lamang nito kay Paeng ang babuyan nila. Kung wala raw siyang mahanap na daga o pusa, malamang nanggagaling ang amoy sa babuyan nila. Pinalinis noon din ni Paeng ang babuyan ngunit hindi pa rin maalis sa ilong niya ang nabubulok na amoy. Nawala na lamang ito nang malanghap niya ang bango ng dama de noche nang may umihip na hangin papasok sa nakabukas na bintana ng kuwarto nila ni Milia.

* * *

Lumalabas na ang mga alitaptap at umiiba na ang tunog sa paligid, ngunit hindi pa rin sila makakita ng rafflesia. Nakapagpasya na ang giyang kapareha ni Paeng kung saan nila itutulos ang kanilang mga tent, nang marinig nila ang mga sigaw. May bahid ng takot ang mga sigaw ngunit halatang pinipilit ng mga itong huwag mataranta. Nanggaling ang mga ito sa dalawang lalaking estudyanteng magkapareha. Pakarinig sa sigaw, lumapit na rin sa giya at kay Paeng sina Mr. Guzman at Omeng.

"May bangkay," sabi ng isa habang nakaturo naman ang daliri ng ikalawa.

Natuwa ang manunulat. Sa wakas, nakakita na rin ng rafflesia. Hindi masasayang ang pag-akyat niya ng Isarog. Ngunit umiling ang dalawang estudyante. Nang dalhin sila ng dalawa sa lugar na itinuturo nila, isang bangkay ng babae ang kanilang nakita. Pinagpipistahan ng mga bangaw ang bangkay. May mga gumagapang na ritong langgam. Nakasuot ito ng maong na putikan. Dikit na dikit sa katawan nito ang suot na t-shirt dahil sa basang kapaligiran. Nakadilat pa ang mata nitong namumutla na. Matigas na ang katawan, sa wari nila. Hindi malayong kapag ginalaw nila ang bangkay, makakakita na sila ng uod. Hindi nila matiyak kung ilang oras o araw na itong nandoon. Ang amoy ng bangkay ang sinundan ng dalawang estudyante. Akala nila rafflesia; nabigla sila nang makatagpo ng bangkay sa gitna ng kagubatan.

Nagkatinginan silang lahat. Natulala pati ang dalawang lalaking unang nakakita sa bangkay. Hanggang sa parang mabagal at tiyak na tikatik ng ulan sa paligid, binasa ang ulo nila at katawan ng larawan ng bangkay na babae, na nakatambad sa harap nila. Tumagos hanggang sa isip nila. Noon nila naramdaman kung paano nadiligan ang kanilang takot, ang kanilang kaba. Una ang takot: umusbong na supling ng apitong na tarantang tumubo papailanlang, naging bantayog sa gitna ng gubat, nag-unat ng mga sanga at naglabas ng mga dahon. Pinanindigan sila ng balahibo. Doon sila kinapitan ng pandududa at pangamba, mga baging na nagunyapit sa katawan nila. Paano kung nasa paligid pa ang pumatay sa babae? Paano kung mapagkamalang sila ang pumatay? Paano nila patutunayan? Paano kung hindi dapat matuklasan ang bangkay? Tiyak madidiyaryo sila. Mababasa ang pangalan nila sa pahayagan. Makikilala sila ng mga pumatay sa babae. Patuloy na lumaki ang takot nila, higit pang yumayabong hanggang sa maglaglagan ang mga dahon nitong nagkapatung-patong sa lupa upang patahanin sila. Pinalambot ng mga dahon ang lupang kinatatayuan nila. Kung kaya walang nalikhang kalabog ang mga bungang ibinagsak ng mga punong patuloy pa rin sa paglaki. Kailangang huwag mataranta. Matatanda na sila. Lahat lalaki. Mangyari na ang mangyayari.

"Kailangang masabihan natin agad ang bantay ng national ng park," mungkahi ni Omeng.

"Kailangan nating bumaba agad at ipaalam ito sa pulis," sang-ayon ng isa sa dalawang lalaking nakatagpo sa bangkay.

"Hindi ko alam ang daan sa gabi. Baka mawala tayo," pagtatapat ng giya.

Napatingin silang lahat sa giya. Hindi sila makapaniwala sa sinabi nito. Hindi nila lubos maisip na matutulog na lamang sila dito samantalang may nakahandusay na bangkay ilang metro lamang ang layo sa kanila. Pakiramdam ng giya bigla na lamang nilusob ng anay ang takot niya. Umumbok ang mga punso sa lupa at sumabog na parang bulkan. Naglabasan ang mga anay. Nagkapakpak ang ilan upang salakayin ang takot ng giya na baka mawala sila sa dilim. Ngunit walang papantay sa tigas at tibay ng apitong. Hindi ito basta-basta na lamang napatutumba ng anay. Walang nagawa ang giya kundi yumuko sa hiya.

Narinig na lamang nilang nagkuwento si Mr. Guzman kahit may pama-hiin itong huwag pag-usapan ang gagawin niyang kuwento hangga't hindi pa naisusulat. Walang hinto ito sa pagkukuwento at wala silang ibang nagawa kundi makinig. Isusulat niya raw na baka kasapi ng NPA ang babae at isinuplong ng kapwa niya kasamahan o ng militar. Baka raw pinatay sa ibang lugar ang babae at doon lamang itinapon. Ngunit higit daw na mag-anda ang kuwento kung matutuklasan nilang isa pala ito sa mga residenteng pumuprotekta sa Bundok ng Isarog. Baka raw may natuklasan itong paki-kipagsabwatan sa pagitan ng DENR at ng mga illegal loggers, kaya siya ipinapatay at itinapon sa bundok para mapagkamalang NPA. Walang hinto si Mr. Guzman sa paggawa ng posibilidad para sa kanyang kuwento. Naramdaman na lamang ni Paeng na nasa tabi na niya si Omeng. Naramdaman na lamang niyang parang binabangungot na naman siyang muli ng pagsabog ng Bundok ng Isarog. Pakiramdam niya'y muli na naman siyang nalulunod. Ngunit ngayo'y hindi na sa tubig kundi sa paligsahang mabuhay ng lahat ng makita niya sa loob ng gubat. Saka umusbong ang mga bulaklak sa paligid. Nagsabog ang mga kulay mula sa pinakamaitim hanggang sa mga kulay ng bahaghari. Naghalu-halo ang mga amoy mula sa pinakamailap hanggang sa pinakamabaho. Binalot ng lumot ang lahat ng bagay mula sa bagong supling hanggang sa nabubulok na bangkay. Iginalang nila ang takot ng bawat isa. Iginala nila sa paligid ang kanilang matang puno ng hiya. Hanggang sa wala na silang pinagkaiba sa mga puno sa loob ng gubat. Nakaugat na sila sa lugar na kinatatayuan nila. Hindi sila makagalaw, parang mga rebultong buhay sa gitna ng kagubatan.

Muling naamoy ni Paeng ang rafflesia na pinagpipistahan ng mga bangaw. Naalala niya kung paano idineklara ni Mr. Guzman na patay na ang may-akda, patay na ang may-akda sa araw na nakapasok ang bangaw sa kabahayan nila ni Milia, na kukuwentuhan ni Paeng pagkababa niya ng Isarog, nang umiiyak at nakayakap sa dibdib ng kanyang asawa, kung paano niya hindi maintindihan ang kasukalan ng kagubatan.

The Beginnings of a Bridge

We believe there is no stopping
civilization, progress by means of

interruptions: leveled mangrove lung,
creek erasures, barred rail eggs beneath

soles of machines. There it is, now half
of a causeway, a horizon wound growing

like gray rot on water, seascape gangrene.
Leviathan reaching out to its twin

on opposite reclaimed shores. Reaching
towards us no matter where we look.

All iron and concrete muscle, it sheds
more and more of itself behind like

perverse flotsam. Or the most menacing
of tails: These are the beginnings of a bridge.

The beginnings of the third that defiles
Tagbilaran Bay: thrice the wreckage of reefs,

thrice the seafolk wonder, *Where to now?*
We make way for the colossal, always,

and tomorrow we might never wake up
to new shadows etched on our land.

Earth Mother

This is a land that consumes her own, a mother
who holds us cradled, pliant at her breast
as she sucks us to the marrow of our essential life.
With her breath, she infuses into our nature
the coarse grains of her earth. Nothing in our bones
will wake, a ghost in the night in windy trees
sighing unearthly music, useless to this world—
pink rose of dawn beyond the lost glades of paradise.
We are her creatures then, bred into our blood
a spreading corruption caught of her earth,
which makes it natural in our throats to force
such sounds up like boars make as we rut for the female
between her limbs—and ruins beyond utterance,
speech that salves mortality in our flesh, our earth.

*The Belly of the Beast*_____

In the ten years that Aman had lived on Estar Island, he knew three things to be true:

> The moon never left the sky.
> The ground was always slightly damp and slippery, despite the grip on his secondhand moss shoes.
> The children were never allowed to go beyond the perimeter of the island.

It was the last one that always chafed at Aman. He wanted to get out there and follow in the footsteps of his father, Artur. His father led the hunting expeditions into the soft caverns that surrounded their little island, the shallow waters forever sloshing against the pebbly shorelines. The hunting expeditions, usually comprising of about seven to ten of their most seasoned explorers, would venture beyond the pale glow of the moon to search for the gifts of the water: wriggling krill as big as Aman's palms; gasping silver fish that could easily feed a family of four; globs of a pale, waxy substance that, when thrown on an open flame, ensured that the fire would continuously burn for days; bundles of seaweed, dark and slippery on the tongue, tasting of the sea.

That was another thing that Aman wanted to see. His grandmother, Lola Tely, said that the sea encompassed the whole world, reaching toward the horizon in a vast, whispering expanse of blue. Aman was confused—the water he knew was dark, tepid, and smelled slightly of piss. It never rose past his ankles and collected in pools around the island. He could never imagine that much water. Lola Tely laughed—she said that the sea was also salty, but not like piss. It had a clean, tangy taste, as though the world were continuously being washed anew.

Artur told his wife's mother to stop filling Aman's head with nonsense.

But when his father was away on a hunting expedition—the Moon-Blessed Priest seemed to be forever at the entrance of their small dome, her pale white finger crooked forward to summon Artur—Lola Tely would pause and gesture for Aman to come closer. They would sit in front of the small, standing furnace, watching the fire leap behind the metal grate, and

Lola Tely would wrap one of her old blankets around Aman's shoulders. The blanket was made out of proper cloth from the Before Times, not like the shoddy secondhand water suits that everyone wore in order to prevent the constant moisture from destroying human skin. The soft weave of the fiber reminded Aman of being cradled in the arms of his mother before she contracted the wasting disease and her body was released beyond the shores of the island. Lola Tely would clear her throat, flex her fingers, pull Aman closer, and tell him a story:

> Long ago, when the sun was still high in the sky, and the moon was buried beneath the deepest ocean, the great beasts of the universe came together to discuss the annihilation of the world.
>
> The Great Goat bleated at the assemblage in front of him. The shadows grew hungrier each day, and soon, there would be nothing left of this world. The next world was far away, a distant dream that the great beasts needed to migrate to. Each beast had the opportunity to save one thing from the universe before the darkness arrived. One by one, each beast declared what they wanted to preserve.
>
> The Phoenix chose fire. The Frog chose the fly. The Spider chose the stalks of wheat waving in the field—

What is wheat? Aman would ask with his fingers.
His grandmother shrugged. *I don't know. I'm only telling you a story.*

> Each beast chose what was most important to them, the single element that they would take into the next universe as the darkness arrived to wipe away the current one, like a wave engulfing the shore. The Hare chose the breeze, while the Water Buffalo chose rain, and the Dragon chose the horizon. The Cat chose the sun. As she stretched her great body, her jaws widened to encircle the bright sphere of light. When she swallowed the sun, the sky was dimly lit by the stars.
>
> The Bakunawa was the last to arrive, and there were slim pickings remaining. Many of the great beasts had already left, shifting away from the shadows that continuously encroached across the land. The Great Goat was calmly chewing cud when the Bakunawa swam up to the shoreline.
>
> *I will choose the moon,* said the Bakunawa.

And that's the same moon outside? Aman would ask in wonderment.
Maybe his grandmother would always sign. *What I know is that this is our moon.*
But what about the other one? The sun?
I guess the Cat did not give it back, Lola Tely would say.
That's mean. And what about us? Which of the great beasts saved us?
I'm getting to that part.

One by one, the great beasts flew and swam and walked away from the world, leaving the remnants of the land to the shadows. There was barely any light left: perhaps one or two of the unclaimed stars, the faint glow of mushrooms and fungi that were left behind. The Bakunawa, swimming on the last of the tides with its fellow sea creatures, thought it heard a song, and paused in its movements.

Come, said the Dolphin and the Whale and the Sea Lion. We will be left behind and the shadows will close in.

But I hear a song—

No, there is no song, they said. Come, Bakunawa, we must leave now. The shadows smell of sorrow and death and decay. We must go.

But the Bakunawa swam up to the nearest shore and found a group of humans there, in their skin suits and portable life domes, carrying their children on their backs. They were the ones singing, their voices coming together as one, casting the chorus into the great ether and hoping for salvation. A child was crying. She was the one who drew the Bakunawa to their group.

The Bakunawa, in its infinite memory, remembered a time when it, too, had a family, when its child cried for milk, when its mate sang the song of the ocean back to them through the ripples of the air. And though it was already carrying the moon inside it, the Bakunawa thought that there might be room for one more piece of this world to be saved.

That's a great story, Lola.

Lola Tely would stroke his hair and cradle his head against the crook of her shoulder. *It's a good story to remember,* she would tell him gently as they both stared at the small flames that continuously burned behind the grate.

When Aman was eleven years old, Lola Tely became violently ill. Her fingers became claws that froze at her sides. She could barely turn her head this way or that, and her eyes became thin slits that sunk into her face. Aman tried to feed her extra nutrient paste beyond her allocation (he sometimes went to sleep with a pang in his stomach, a growing blackness much like the shadows surrounding the moon), but she could barely swallow it.

Artur went in and out of their dome, consulting with the Moon-Blessed Priest and her cadre of healers, and came back with liniments and oils that smelled foul and nauseating to Aman. But he still rubbed the oils on Lola Tely's hands, trying to get her fingers to unclench, and massaged the liniments on her bone-thin limbs, unwrapping her arms and legs from the blankets one section at a time so that she would not feel the cold.

But it did little good. Her skin was cool and dry, despite their attempts at letting her sweat out the sickness. Her body shook with phantom pains, and her lips became as dry as the remnants of the fire that littered the bottom of their small furnace. Aman was not sure if his grandmother could still hear him, but he whispered stories to her late at night, when his father was away for the hunt. (How much could he hunt? Aman thought bitterly. Shouldn't he be here, with his wife's mother, sheltering her toward her final slumber?) Aman did not know the rituals of death; he was too young to participate in them when his own mother passed, but he remembered story and song and the passing of the carved bone cups that they said came from beyond the moon. He remembered his grandmother's stories about the sea and felt his heart sink like a stone.

He woke up to the moon's pale glow, seeping between the gaps of their dome and bathing their home in a silver light. The furnace had gone low, and the single-round room was cold. Lola Tely was curled up like a stone in front of the dying furnace, in a pile of warm things: her water suit was beneath her house suit, which was beneath her hunting suit, which was beneath her blankets from the Before Times. Aman moved to open the furnace door to awaken the dormant flame, but was stopped by a clawed hand reaching out to him. His grandmother wrapped her stiffening fingers around his wrist, her mouth opening as if to say something.

And then she took a breath.

And another.

And then stopped breathing forever.

Aman crouched down in front of Lola Tely's body. Her fingers were still warm around his bare skin, and he could feel her nails digging into the soft flesh of his wrist. He thought about her stories—about the Great Bakunawa who turned back and rescued them in the Before Times, before the world ended. He could imagine its long, low song vibrating across the last of the stars, its body blocking out the last of the light. He wondered how true the story was; his father had always reminded him that stories were for the women, to occupy their minds and their homes while the men hunted and kept them safe. Aman wished that he could create new stories and tell new tales. Aman wished that he could have his grandmother back.

When Artur returned from his hunt, he found his son and his wife's mother side by side near an unlit furnace. The faint smell of smoke hung in the air. One of the bodies lay still; the other continued to breathe. If he said a prayer of gratitude, nobody heard it—except, perhaps, the moon, which hung, ever-steady, in the darkening sky.

Aman awoke to the sound of whispers. He was alone in their dome. His water suit clung to his body like a second skin, and he wished nothing more than to strip the black-and-gray material off. For a moment, he thought that he could hear his grandmother's voice among the waves of voices, but the moment passed as he gained consciousness. It had been several cycles since Lola Tely's body had been sent back to the water and her material possessions redistributed to the other members of the community. These days, Aman could barely remember what it felt like to hold her hand or to feel her arms around his shoulders in companionable warmth. He had just turned twelve and was no longer considered a child. Today was the first day that he was required to apprentice with his father to learn the ways of the hunt.

Softly, Aman crept around the shadowy dome. Their fuel shares had been reduced as soon as Lola Tely died, which meant that they now had to do many of their tasks by moonlight or by touch since the furnace could no longer be used for light or to warm the dome as often as before. Aman automatically bundled his sleeping materials and shoved them to the side, making sure to carefully keep his grandmother's blanket hidden from his father. It was the only thing he had that belonged to her. Artur would probably make him give it up to the Moon-Blessed Priest, saying that it would become one of those sacrifices that she demanded from the community every cycle.

As he strapped his survival kit across his waist, Aman felt a fire in his chest. He fed that fire with anger and resentment, with bitterness and grief, like too much fuel in a too-small furnace. He wanted to scream at his father, to smash his hunting weapons and his lumensticks, to take a blade to the face of the Moon-Blessed Priest for filling his father's head with lies about how they would soon find a land where the moon did not hang in the sky eternally, where the land was dry and sweet, and where the water was clear, fresh, and cool. Unlike Lola Tely, the old Moon-Blessed Priest did not allow anyone else to ask questions about her stories (*What happened to…?*), let any of them express doubt (*How did the moon bless her in the first place?*), or even interrupt her for clarifications (*What does it mean when you say…?*). She just spoke on and on, raising her bundle of lumensticks to the moon, and her sycophants and followers just nodded silently in agreement. None of them ever used their hands to speak, only their mouths, and only when permitted. Aman did not want to become like his father or the other men and women who followed the Moon-Blessed Priest.

No, he wanted to follow his own path.

With the feeling of fire and frustration still in his chest, Aman moved toward the entrance of their dome, where the whispers were becoming louder, until Aman could string together the meaning of words.

"… we must think about the survival of the island." It was the soft, melodious voice of the Moon-Blessed Priest.

"We cannot cull all the elderly!" Artur's voice rose above the rustling voices.

"Why not?" asked someone else. "You allowed us to do that to your wife's mother."

Aman's heart turned from fire to ice as the words ran through his body.

"That was different," Artur said. "She was filling my son's head with nonsense. It had to stop."

"The moon has spoken to me in my dreams. Supplies are running out, and we must ensure that only the healthiest and strongest survive until we reach our destination," interceded the Moon-Blessed Priest. "We thank you for your sacrifice, Manong Artur. I hope that it shows the others what a model member of our community looks like."

Several voices spoke at once, their words tangling around each other like seaweed. Aman slowly backed away from the entrance, his feet sliding quietly across the damp ground. He needed to tell the others. At the opposite end of the dome, there was a small gap between the ground and the frame. When Aman was small, he could easily wriggle beneath the space. He hoped that he was still thin enough to escape.

In the flickering light of his last lumenstick, Aman crouched beneath a large, wobbling overhang, making sure to keep the glow partially hidden in the curve of his body. He could no longer hear the squelching sounds of footsteps following him. In fact, he could no longer hear much of anything: beyond the glow of the moon and the raised, spongy hillocks of the island, there were pockets of silence where nobody except the hunters would regularly traverse. But beyond the usual hunting grounds, Aman knew nothing about shadows.

And now he was surrounded by them.

He cupped the lumenstick in his palms, humming one of Lola Tely's old songs softly under his breath as he tried to calm himself. He knew they would be looking for him after what he said to their community, and if they found him, his father would lose another family member to the Moon-Blessed Priest. But where would he go? There was nothing else but the everlasting moon, the dome, Estar Island—everything else were simply stories.

Hum, hummm, hummmmm—

Aman felt the sound rather than heard it: a sound deep in his belly, vibrating through his feet and hands, and shaking his entire body. He looked around, pressing his back against the soft, curved cavern wall behind him and slipping his lumenstick into his survival kit to tamp the light. But there was nobody around. And yet, the sound. The sound!

Hum, hummm, hummmmm—

It filled his entire body, grasping each nerve ending and lighting them up so that his skin felt as though it tingled all over. The sound seemed to come from the walls, the ground, and the curved ceiling of the cavern, shaking the entire space. Aman closed his eyes and began humming the song again. He felt the sound sink into the melody coming from his mouth, as though it were a twin sound emerging from the very bottom of the earth. Pressing one palm against the cavern wall, Aman began walking toward the source of the sound.

Hum, hummm, hummmmm—

Keeping his eyes closed, Aman allowed the sound to guide his footsteps. He felt the soft ground slowly angling upward, the cavern wall unevenly pulsing beneath his palm. Soon, the wall gave way to wetness, and a strange cold feeling enveloped Aman's bare hands and neck.

He opened his eyes to a strange sight: his left palm was resting on a pale-colored rock, hard and unyielding. Where Estar Island and the surrounding caverns were porous and slick, this was thick and tough and ended on a sharp point. As he turned his head, he realized that he was looking at rows upon rows of the same sharp rocks, jagged and uneven. And though the ground was still soft and familiar, Aman gaped at the height and majesty of the new sight.

It was then that he realized that the sound had stopped. Instead, an ear-splitting moan washed over Aman as he felt the ground give way beneath his feet, the rock formations suddenly shifting from vertical to horizontal, his understanding of up and down changing as his entire being tumbled all the way down. His fingers grasped nothing but a slippery surface that shifted up and down, like waves across the surface of a pond.

As he fell into nothingness, his body about to meet the pale, sharp tips of the stone that had just, moments ago, guided him to this place, Aman looked up. His eyes, long used to the dim light of the forever moon, could scarcely understand the sight in front of him:

In the distance, two sinuous beings were moving towards each other. One had glinting scales that seemed to be made of water, its jaws open as it released the horizon. The other, softly moving across the darkness, its soft body arching as it tilted its head upwards and released the sun.

Clouded Eyes in Paradise_____

I recall my first encounter with a snake as an old memory from my childhood. This was during a class excursion to the zoo in my early primary school days, when I was barely ten. A humongous reptiliasn, its girth wider than the size of my head, was hoisted from a rattan basket and onto the back of a man's neck. The buttery-looking reptile remained still.

A long snaking queue was formed, with excited guests eagerly waiting for their first possible experience with the impressive constrictor and organic yellow-white swirls stamped across its massive coils. This was the albino-Burmese python. Despite feeling a strong sense of apprehension, I stood in line with the rest of the class, determined to participate. Strangely enough, the wait was filled with anxiety, and I could almost feel the fear permeating through my skin even before I set my gaze upon the cold-blooded creature. As the snake drew closer, I could feel my heart beat accelerating and thumping frantically against my ribcage. My hands were icy cold. Finally, it was my turn. I took a deep breath and gave its thick, scaly body a firm poke. A wave of disgust crawled over my entire back like an electric shock, sending me scurrying away from the beast as I quivered in revulsion. What was that?

In hindsight, the fear probably stemmed from my inability to comprehend what was in front of me. Was I supposed to be afraid? Was that *thing* dangerous? I had no idea. Growing up, there was an absence of adult role models to teach me about my relationship with nature. The occasional amusing walks in parks were all I knew. I remembered my family's strong refusal to enter the boardwalk at the Lower Pierce Reservoir Trail the moment they read the informative signage describing the different snake species one might bump into. That memory had left a lasting imprint in my psyche, reinforcing the belief that snakes are indeed *frightening* and should be feared.

*

In Southeast Asia, our survival is heavily intertwined with agricultural production, and our ancestors have long looked to snakes as powerful ecological indicators of the rice harvest. These slender beauties have long held great significance in many folk tales. In Java, Indonesia, there is the story of

Dewi Sri, daughter of Sri Mahapungun, who was asked by King Pulagra for her hand in marriage. She refused to marry and wished to escape, and the gods, hearing of her plight, took pity and transformed her into an enormous snake of the paddy fields—*Ular Sawah*, the reticulated python. The tale ends with her death, her body manifesting in all things fertile—a variety of seeds, among them of which was rice.[1]

Within the paddy fields, pythons are natural keepers of the crops. Their form allows them to be nimble among the dense vegetation, and they are swift at weeding out rats and other vermin. Snakes, protector of human sustenance, were celebrated as a symbol of fertility and growth, strongly echoing the vitality of nature.

*

There is a wide spectrum of emotional responses people might have to snakes, either triggered by our natural responses to danger or influences from cultural beliefs and narratives. One of the more common emotional responses is fear. Physiologically, fear is an instinctive behavior that safeguards us from unknown dangers. Our human brains have been hardwired to quickly detect objects that evoke fear—fast-moving salient stimuli—and that includes snakes.[2] However, fear does not equate to evil, and we should untangle the connection between the two.

Today, our relationship with snakes has been clouded by the way popular culture and narratives misrepresent them as emblems of evil with malevolent intentions. This has intensified our deep-rooted fears of snakes. Perhaps it is time to question the way serpents are understood and misunderstood and reframe their place in the world.

Most would be familiar with the classic Greek mythology of the snake-haired Gorgon lady.[3] She was a daughter of Phorcys and Ceto, more famously known as Medusa. Ferocious, evil, and hateful, she petrifies those who caught her gaze, turning them into lifeless stone statues. But why and how was she adorned with these scales of *wickedness*? Tragically for Medusa, she was sexually assaulted by the sea god Poseidon in the temple of Athena. As punishment for staining the sacredness of her temple, Athena transformed Medusa's beautiful, luscious hair into terrifying, wriggling snakes. The sea god Poseidon saw little to no consequences for his actions.

These ancient narratives have quietly glissaded their way into contemporary times. The notion of slaying a Gorgon parallels the way we condone violent snake extirpation as a heroic act where human good triumphs serpentine evil. But when I see Perseus holding Medusa's head aloft in triumphant victory, I see her crown held in painful bondage by a man who knew nothing of her life, the matted coils of rageful and hissing serpents who did nothing to deserve their fate, her face written in the language of anguish and despair, of someone who never had a voice.

Judgments are easily cast upon snakes based on their seemingly menacing demeanors, with hardly a thought given to understanding them as they truly are. Society is naturally attracted to the charismatic. We adore the doe-eyed, furry, and feathery creatures that we can more easily relate to, viewing them as good, while we label what we do not understand as evil. This lack of empathy and understanding toward less charismatic creatures is apparent and, in fact, cruel. The creatures less likeable in the eyes of society are often unaccepted and mistreated, sculpted into evil emblems through the skewed lens of human misunderstanding. Should we not instead cultivate a deeper sense of appreciation for all creatures and beings in this world, accepting that each has its reason to exist on equal grounds with one another?

Perhaps, as we shed our ignorance, we will begin to see emblems of evil, like snakes and Medusa, as misunderstood beings with their own stories to tell.

*

Water has long been essential for life. Developed cities are often depleted of natural freshwater networks like rivers and streams. In these types of environments with highly modified landscapes, carefully designed hydrological systems have since replaced the role of natural waterways. Structures like canals, sewage, and drains, form an intricate web of life for snakes, particularly the reticulated python, to travel around and thrive in our urban ecosystems.[4]

Serpents in Singapore are well adapted to our urban hydrological infrastructure. Their serpentine form allows them to cruise unimpeded through small pathways like shallow drains and water pipes, and most importantly, the major expressways—our monsoon canals. This makes maneuvring and searching for food highly convenient across the labyrinth of water networks in the city.

Drain-cology is a term I fondly coined in my studies to describe the snake's inextricable relationship with moist and dark underground tunnels, a safe retreat hidden in plain sight. A majestic guardian of Hindu mythology, a primordial being of creation,[5] a slithering scaly traveler of forested greens and flowing rivers, serpents in the well-known public consciousness today have become splendid survivors of habitat loss. They have since assumed the roles of the elusive protectors of underground dungeons that traverse the spaces beneath our feet—pythons, for instance, are natural pest controllers; their ability to keep vermin populations low prevents the spread of vector diseases.[6] There is something quite breath-taking and charming in the snake's resilience and ability to assimilate to change.

When I first learned of this, I felt a rushing sense of awe toward the snake's glorious reclamation of its identity. Reticulated pythons, the longest snake on earth, play a significant role within the socio-ecological ecosystem, as evidenced by their interactions within their immediate spatial geography.

I drew a connection between the pythons of our city and the Nāgas (divine snake-like beings inspired by the likeness of cobras) of the sacred groves of India's Western Ghats. Highly revered and feared in equal measure, these serpent deities are regarded as spiritual guardians of the groves and their environs.[7] The exploration of our contemporary story is just an iteration of ancient narratives.

A great deal of biodiversity has persisted in these well connected but scarcely lit tunnels, resulting in the existence of interdependent living. Various creatures have built well-camouflaged homes, traveling silently through them and living and dying heroically away from our watchful eyes. The tunnels present a vast array of wildlife on a platter for the serpents, from croaking frogs and toads to scuttling lizards and geckos to squeaky rats and more. Imagine that ribbon-like tongue flickering in the dark in anticipation.

Now, picture nature's clean-up crew live in action. A feisty equatorial spitting cobra gave chase, biting down on the soft amphibious body with accuracy, delivering a generous dose of lethal venom. On the other end of the canal, a muscular reticulated python is tracking down a vermin's scent, ready for an ambush, when suddenly, a whiff of a chubby feline gives it pause.

Much of these action-packed hunts are well concealed from public scrutiny, happening in the depths of the underground Waterway Obscura. Evidently, our snakes thrive with enormous success in our hydrological systems, reflective of their toughness and flexibility in adapting to urbanization in Singapore.

*

Fast forward fourteen years later, and I find myself actively involved in many hectic wildlife rescue operations with the Animal Concerns Research and Education Society on a weekly basis. I have had many life-changing encounters with all sorts of wildlife, including the subject of this essay, whom I have grown to admire. In this work, it feels as though I have been given a second chance to re-encounter the snake and to repent for the first time I met and poked its scaly body. I felt my calling to fiercely guard and protect these lustrous creatures from the dangers of society and from unfounded misconceptions and hostility.

On one of my scorching afternoon shifts, the rescue mobile phone rang incessantly during our short-lived lunch break. The panicky caller alerted us to a "devious-looking rope" found hanging on his clock. It was full-on paparazzi—the sinuous creature was photographed from all possible angles, and these shots were sent to the rescue hotline. "Please come quickly," he pleaded.

Snakes can pick up on the tension emitted by fearful human beings. They might resort to defensive measures if our movements are uncertain or perceived as threatening to them, which, in turn, makes them unpredictable. When handling a snake, it is essential to keep it cool and collected.

This small window of interaction is a game changer, both for the snake and the caller. In this short time, my actions could either subvert the caller's misconceptions about snakes or reinforce them. Failure to convince and assure the caller that the snake meant no serious harm and was merely looking for some geckos as food or for some respite in his home would mean another intolerant or misinformed citizen. It would mean a missed opportunity to educate society about snakes and prevent their ruthless extermination on sight.

So, no more shudders or squirms this time. With my left hand offering gentle support and a firm grip on the right, I picked up the Paradise Tree Snake and reeled it closer to my body, reassuring it with my warmth. Flaunting its crawling skills as an arboreal serpent, it glided seamlessly across my neck and eventually settled on my back as its stable perch.

This display of gentle, nonverbal interaction reassured the caller like a warm embrace. He inched forward with interest to catch a closer glimpse of this tender moment. His curiosity about snakes piqued after this mini-escapade, which sowed seeds of positive change in his heart. Many months later, I received a text from him that read "Beautiful day to sun tan," accompanied by an endearing shot of a Paradise Tree snake fully relaxed on a branch, soaking up the lovely morning rays.

*

As we slither in between the old folklore and new-found stories in search of the serpent's sublime charm, we should recognize how snakes are impressive and important ecological conduits, playing a vital role in our environment. They also serve as a mirror for how we treat the less understood. It is time to leave our old stories of the vile serpent behind. Instead, let us awaken into new skins of understanding and new scales of knowledge and growth.

November 20, 2018, 9 p.m. Under the tropical humidity of concrete streets and piercing white street lights, a reticulated python was resting beneath the shallow drains. The iron bars of the drain cover cast harsh shadows on the beady, motionless skin of the reptile's body. It was still, as if it were holding its breath, awaiting judgment from the fearsome crowd that had gathered around the scene: the cold white body of a white tabby cat, lying nearby lifeless on the grey concrete floor.

Murder was written in red by the suffocating strangles around the neck, splattered on its pure white coat. The python knew not, but it had committed the crime of hunting a forbidden prey and is now at the mercy of an angry mob, even though it had hunted as it always had for millennia. Though unaware of the sins it has committed in a strange world it knew not, it awaits its trial.

*

Yet again, this became one of the many twisted struggles and strangling conflicts between humans and wildlife inflicted by fundamental misunderstandings of our natural ecosystems. Our current paradigm brings humanity further from empathy, disconnecting us from our natural world by clouding hearts and minds, perpetuating fear and ignorance in an endless nightmare, feeding on itself like an ouroboros.

When will we be able to wrench the tail from the mouth and truly learn to coexist with nature?

NOTES

1. Wessing, Robert. "Sri and Sedana and Sita and Rama: Myths of Fertility and Generation." *Asian Folklore Studies*, vol. 49, no. 2, 1990, p. 235, DOI: 10.2307/1178035.

2. Isbell, Lynne A. "Snakes as Agents of Evolutionary Change in Primate Brains." *Journal of Human Evolution*, vol. 51, no. 1, July 1, 2006, pp. 1–35, www.sciencedirect.com/science/article/pii/S0047248406000182 (accessed March 28, 2023), DOI: 10.1016/j.jhevol.2005.12.012.

3. The Editors of Encyclopedia Britannica. "Medusa | Greek Mythology." *Encyclopædia Britannica*, February 14, 2018, www.britannica.com/topic/Medusa-Greek-mythology.

4. Low, Mary-Ruth. *Global Reintroduction Perspectives: 2018*. Edited by Pritpal S. Soorae, 6th ed., vol. 6, Arafah Printing Press LLC, Abu Dhabi, UAE, IUCN/SSC Reintroduction Specialist Group & Environment Agency-Abu Dhabi, 2018, pp. 93–96, iucn-ctsg.org/project/global-reintroduction-perspectives-2018/ (accessed March 28, 2023).

5. *Shri Sheshanarayana, Vishnu Narayana on Shesha*, 1886, www.metmuseum.org/art/collection/search/78252 (accessed April 9, 2023). Image: 19 1/8 × 14 in. (48.6 × 35.6 cm) Sheet: 20 × 14 in. (50.8 × 35.6 cm).

6. Low. *Global Reintroduction Perspectives*.

7. Landry Yuan, Félix, et al. "Sacred Groves and Serpent-Gods Moderate Human–Snake Relations." *People and Nature*, vol. 2, no. 1, November 24, 2019, pp. 111–122, DOI: 10.1002/pan3.10059.

CHOO YI FENG

We Don't Sleep at Night_____

MORNING, HIGH TIDE, WAXING CRESCENT.

There is a flower on his chest. He looks down at it, tilting his head against the tug of the earth, his back pressed against the squelch of soft mud. Its petals are limp, flaccid, flesh-like, and delicate, trapped in an envelope of tidal pool left behind as the sea drops them upon the cot of this scarred edge of a shore. The sky is gray with clouds that won't rain; there are no humans in sight, though a great many beasts with black feathers fill the skies. His arms bud out from his torso, limbs finding the human shape of fingers that curiously tickle the edges of these blossoming entrails sprouting from his chest, feeling them tremble as they tuck themselves back into the cavity of his bloodless chest, so that all that remains is a tuft like chest hair. All around him, carried in by the waves, is garbage piled high into towers, drifting on pungent sea-foam like dead bodies that will not rot.

By then, we had all heard of the stories, of course, fed to children at night in place of meals, our stomachs brimming with folklore and groaning for more. Children who wandered where they were told it was not safe were swept out to sea by the hiss and crackle of flash floods, tropical storms, and rip currents that took our frail bodies to flay upon tired boulders. Skulls cracked, bones ground to dust—all that was left of us were our souls, and even those were not spared; the jelly-eyed phantoms far out beyond sucked them up like nutrient broths, as were the sea witches who had devised means to capture drowned souls, all the better to gild their throats with so that their silken songs could pull yet more sailors to their graves.

In those early moments, he bears the flower in his chest like a wound, gasping for air when he does not need any, keeping the tissue moist. He steps on soft mud that hugs him from the spaces between his toes, oozing brine with every landing of his footfalls. The black crows take notice, shadowing him from a cautious distance, hungry for food but unable to recognize that damp flesh of his. He searches for signs of human life and finds none, but sees how bristle worms, lokan clams, and siput unam emerge from the wake of his footsteps, like flowers disturbed too early from a teeming ground.

128

If it was true that children who wandered too far—although by then his was not quite the body of a boy but of a small malnourished man—were taken into the depths of the sea, made playthings of by invisible monsters, then he might have fallen into the interstices, tossed onto a nobody's beach to be forgotten to time. Neither alive enough to be dead nor dead enough to lose the whole, lose this aching awareness of the piercing cry of a life on its last lap.

EVENING, EBB TIDE, WAXING GIBBOUS.

He comes to learn that the bones of his new home are erected on the shell of the old world. What had once been disordered clumps of nondescript waste began to take on familiar shapes—here is where the school used to be, and there is the shrine where they made their offerings. His own home—nowhere, buried, excavated, a scratch in the dirt rubbed out, lost. When the sun is setting, he scrambles up a little hill, almost falling, cutting himself against junkyard shrapnel. He catches glimpses of the abandoned telecommunications tower where the winged creatures make their nests, a skeleton of rusted steel papered over in plastic ephemera that serves as bedding for soft eggs and fervent hatchlings.

From here, he watches the embers of forest fires eating their way through the horizon, the vehement brilliance of gas flares burning the night out of the sky. At the loneliest hours, the waves follow suit with their own sparkling displays, heaving sea fireflies in their hundreds upon the tidal flats that flicker with luminous agitation; their electric blue discharges a display of excitement and exhaustion. Oceanic will o' the wisps, he finds himself drawn to the ephemeral beauty of these ostracods, the way they compose shapes out of his inky reflection, shapes that look familiar and taunt him with lapsed tragedies. He sleeps in a den woven from compacted sand and refuse, concealed from the phantasmal half-night of this parody of darkness.

He finds himself avoiding daylight, but unacquainted with these ghastly sensations of nighttime. Mornings and evenings, the phases of transition, are the times when he is most active, foraging on the shore, pushing his buoyant raft out into the cold water, and furnishing the husk where he resides. His skin is now drenched in the crushed powder of ostracod carcasses harvested from the strand line, his lithe body luminescent with a galaxy of dying stars. The tide ebbs, and he descends with it, searching the shore for ingredients of literacy: the shell of a paper nautilus, the squishy bodies of sea pens, the ink sacs of cuttlefish, and the chalk of pearly cuttlebones—the things he believes were denied to him in his earlier life. He catalyzes them with sea firefly powder, their staccato glows marking the first and most reliable of transmutations.

The shore shifts like sand grains over furious eddies that catch him in their orbit. One such riptide is different from the others; it reaches in and tugs at the lining of his abdomen, a change so subtle but engulfing him with a feverish force. He stops in the middle of crushing shells, inhaling deeply through his nose. There it is: the scent of a warm body.

LATE AFTERNOON, LOW TIDE, THIRD QUARTER.

Of course, the coast was not truly abandoned—how could we afford to? It had merely been slated for redevelopment, marked with pencils and satellite grids, and allowed to run fallow for a few cycles before the construction projects returned to engineer newer, shinier facades. Surgically, the land and sea were divided with the technical purity of zonations—the core zone, the boundary zone, the unregulated zone, and so on—and in this way, the village settlements, the refugee camp, and other drifters that had once resided there were unwritten.

The first whisperings of trouble had begun seeping out, suggesting that perhaps the rumors and wives' tales were not simple fabrications and that there was in fact something unaccounted for amid the shame-ridden junk heap of our industrial world.

It is on the rotting skeleton of a pier where the first of the patrols sees him—a lithe, supple man of slight build, standing naked above the brown water, his body gleaming from some excess moisture. As they approach, the unmarked being is spooked and slips soundlessly into the water.

Oh, the aroma is so decadent, ripe with possibilities, intermingling with the smells of dried urine, melting plastic, and residual gunpowder. It dances in the air, and even the crows know it; they caw out to one another in fear and excitement for what is about to happen. He can't fall asleep; poison floods the ducts of his body in anticipation. But he must bide his time, knowing it is dangerous to take them both at once.

The younger man, blunt, brash, and built like a bull, is the first to discover the den. He finds a compact mound that is equal parts sand and garbage and ducks under a shred of tarp into a glistening tunnel. It is warm here, but uncomfortably so; the air is stale and sapped of oxygen. His rifle feels slick and achingly dense, its weight pulling at his shoulders and his hips with every step.

He wipes off the oil dripping onto his forehead and emerges into an intimate chamber. A great bulbous cyst is suspended above the ground by a mass of twangy filaments anchored to the ceiling and walls, creating superhighways for scrabbling sea cockroaches. He is overwhelmed by the smell of seaweed and rotting squid and finds himself first suppressing the urge to vomit and then feeling the unexpected, turgid pressure of his erection pressed up against his abdomen underneath his trousers. Plastic rustling within alerts him to something alive; he can't help but imagine the great cyst pulsating with some forbidden secret, that if he were to split its membrane with the point of his rifle, it would moan and tear open to release some kind of foul fetal creature. Childishly, he tests the tension of the sinew nearest to him, wondering if he should, and realizes that the sinews are similarly woven from plastic waste, coated in a milky, waxen film.

Then he hears a whisper of his name. The older man, the sergeant, is lying on the ground on the far side, his rifle missing and his left arm reduced to a stump, his chest dark with blood.

Get out of here, he croaks. Get help. Quickly, before it comes back.

The soldier ignores him, hands trembling as he tries to get the sergeant into a standing position, but is afraid to jostle him because the very solidity of his body feels tenuous. The dripping. There is so much blood. The pungent odor intensifies; brine-rot, seaweed, the husks of prawns, and desiccating squid mixed with the ferric tang of blood spill everywhere, and this time, as it wafts into the air, something warm and damp bursts and leaks into the space between the soldier's legs, even as he tries to lift his comrade's dense, melting form.

Stop. It hurts.

The soldier, trembling, puts down his rifle, adjusts his crotch, and closes his eyes to say a quick prayer before trying one more time. When he opens them again, the sergeant is not the sergeant, and the sharp points of the envenomed claws sink into the juicy pulp of his throat.

MORNING, FLOOD TIDE, FIRST QUARTER.

He no longer powders himself with the residue of sea fireflies, his skin embalmed always in a shimmering, sticky biofilm, its fluorescence its own. His raft was shattered long ago by a rogue storm, and so he takes to the sea with only his body and a salvaged oil drum. There he floats for days at a time, singing to the invisible migrating meroplankton that are drawn to his arms and bones, which plant their seeds in his epidermis and build colonies of wispy hydroids and encrusting barnacles. Polychaetes sleep in the crevices of their ears and backside. Isopods nest in the wiry mass of his pubic hairs. These are the weird, the starving, and the persistent left behind in the wake of destruction, when all the technicolor of sharks, dolphins, and turtles has faded. They, in their facelessness, limblessness, and multi-limbed manyness, are the kin that he makes out here.

He knows that his actions are not in defense of the shoreline. He feels no affiliation with that shell of the old world, thrust into its bleary, indifferent eddies. He knows that they will keep coming, with their survey drones, assault rifles, and armored vehicles. And if they persist for much longer, he will have to relinquish his hold and leave behind the plastic cyst and the dozen corpses of men that he has made a shrine to within the den. Their organs and carcasses no longer serve him any use because the jellyfish gonads that he stews them in are nowhere to be found. The seasonal flush and fallow of their mushrooming masses are not privy to him anymore, and so those bodies and their parts accumulate and rot, a pitiful waste of fresh material.

And he, in turn, lies and soaks here, meditating upon this doubled-over destruction, this cyclical hum of the over-again. In spite of his physiology, his chest rises and falls like the coming and going of waves, stray thoughts breaking against the strand line of his mind and heaving up a miasma of neglected emotions. The realization that he is a shapeshifter; he has to be. He has to find ways to love in the dark and to harbor intimacy with new words.

He has died many times. His spare frame is no match against guns, grenades, and biceps fattened on field rations and pumped iron. A bullet blows out the back of his head, an explosion engulfs him in flames, and the mean edge of a black battle boot severs his spinal cord. Each time it happens the splintered millions of his body scream and fade until the beam of a full moon rising stitches him back together. When he is reassembled, he finds a golf ball lodged in his temporal fossa. A straw sticking out of his appendix. Saran wraps it interlaced with his vertebra. All the oceanic dredge that intermingles.

He thinks about the flower of flesh that sprouted from his chest, the slackness of its mass, and the way it lumps and sags as if punctured, deprived of the amniotic caress of water. He wonders if he can leave. He wonders what else waits for him out in the sea, beyond the confines of this interface, and what hidden and volatile truths buoy his existence here that he might soon perturb.

EVENING, LOW TIDE, FULL MOON.

His severed head, made into a game of football by his long-departed killers, was left wedged in a corner at the mouth of the den, separated from the rest of his bits. At once, it sprouts the scrabbly, hydraulic legs of a coconut crab, carrying him back inside to join the rest of him.

There is another man inside, the most recent soldier, kept feverishly alive, just barely, by infection and microdoses of tetrodotoxin. But his bindings weaken at last, just as the full moon creeps in, releasing him into a nightmare world. When his body comes back to him, he feels the rawness of his skin, stripped of his uniform, as have the carcasses of the other soldiers, suspended in the air, impaled on steel wiring, slack-jawed, eyeless, stump-blackened remainders. He knows he has to leave to get help, but he is still doubled over in agony, his lungs and ribs on fire, his limbs gnarled and defunct. As he lies there on the ground amid the shrine of decay, he eyes the floor and how the coconut crab-head scurries across it and joins the shifting, gelatinous mass of viscera, severed limbs, and mutilated entrails.

The witch is tall and lanky; his hips are too wide, and his neck is too long. His skin is dark and waxy, coated in algae and biofilm that shimmers despondently in the den's half-light. Sticky, clear mucous sloughs off his form in handfuls, a baby's pacifier lodged inside his shoulder, isopods tracing circles around his navel and around his nipples. His genitals are heavy and pendulous with every step. He kneels down and touches his mouth to the soldier's tenderly, as if trying to nibble the softness of his lips away. Almost immediately, the envenomed pain recedes, his nerves tighten, and his flesh returns to him. The soldier smells it immediately. Mossy seaweed, brine rot, squid ink, bile. He is surprised to find that he is rock hard.

The witch has thought about, of course, the possibility of substituting semen for blood in his spells. He thinks about the fishy residue it leaves on his upper lip, the salty tang of it warm on the tongue, the way sperm in their millions erupt frantically, the wasteful plenitude of it all—a recapitulation of clouds of planktonic spawn ejected into the open ocean, their fates open to circulating currents.

The soldier leans in for another kiss, harder this time. The great plastic cyst has been slashed open, spilling heavy innards of failed concoctions and folk tales—a last and desperate attempt to excise the demon from this cursed coast. Their bodies twist and roll over the leather of its depleted membrane as they mate, overcome by a false hunger. There is a strangeness to the witch's flesh that makes the soldier feel like he is fucking the ocean itself, and he succumbs to its delirium, having forgotten what the sea promises.

Outside the den, crows swirl in their rummaging flocks, their lungs scarified by the plumes of char coming from forest fires somewhere beyond. It is clarity that we have now, of all the noise that clouds the sea, oil tankers and piledrivers, and sand barges weaving sonic mirages of islands. The scarlet beads of lasers closing in on him, the palpable unreachability of an orgasm. Luminous hazes are riven by halogen lighting, a glare that drowns out the dance of the ostracod family. We don't sleep at night, even if our bejeweled bodies are still capable of flushing from liquid pleasure.

He feels the full moon and how it swirls and tucks the sea back into a modest package. The low-water mark a line in the sand, and even here, at the edge spaces of ruins, there is an intricacy, a feltness to the coastal crumble. Before daylight comes, the waves swallow us whole with a swollen sigh. There will be a time for this son yet.

*I Should Have Named My Daughter Kaduk*_____

I don't remember the name of the flower I named my daughter after. Which means I don't remember my daughter's name anymore. I don't know if it still grows wild anywhere in Singapore. I don't think it does. I don't see anything growing wild along the grass patches and trees that line every road I walk along when I take my nightly walks. I don't see the thin curls and wisps of *kenanga* petals or the pinwheels of a *kemboja*, nor do I smell the fragrance of *melati*. My daughter says that I'm just being silly, that of course such things still grow in Singapore, and that she's seen them herself. I don't remember her name, so I don't respond.

I no longer sleep at night. Not that time has much meaning for me anymore. Not at my old age and not now, with my memory failing me more with each day. I know I have sons, but I don't know how many. I have a daughter. I don't remember her name. The days blur into each other, and the nights startle me. They come out of nowhere. My block doesn't receive any west sun, which must have been great when my late husband and I first moved in here all those years ago, but now it bothers me that the blocks that surround mine shield me from the natural light of the setting sun. I can never anticipate when the sun might be setting or when the moon might be starting to make its slow, translucent ascent across the pale pink of the sunset before it shines brightly in the blue-black sea of the night. I only know it is night when suddenly it is dark, and instead of feeling sleepy, I get restless. I can't sleep at night. Not anymore.

A young girl sleeps inside me. I don't know who she is. Maybe she is me. I only see her on nights when I close my eyes to try and sleep, and instead of the familiar shower of dots and colors, I see her lying down, facing away from me. She gets the sleep that I don't. I sleep during the day when I make my slow walk down to the dialysis center, and they hook me up to the machine. I don't know how it works. I only know that it takes my blood out and puts it back in. I hear it. It sounds like the waves that I once heard from my village near the coasts of old Singapore. I don't know where the village would be now. I don't know if it would still be on the water. My blood moves in waves in and out of me. I hear my blood flow out of me, and I imagine the waves being pulled away from the shoreline by the power of the moon, and I hear them come back into me in relentless surges, crashing on the shores of my body, before they pull away again. And it repeats. Again and again. Pulling and crashing, ebbing and flowing, the moon yanking it back gently by its foam that gathers on its surface like dispersed clouds before sending it back into me in waves that break on the sand in my mind. I fell asleep to this sound as a child. I can only fall asleep to it now.

* * *

My kids don't understand. I don't know how many kids I have. My daughter gets upset. She tells me not to go "wandering around" at night. I'm not wandering, I tell her. I know where I'm going. I go to the canals and longkangs and hope that there is rain that day. If there was, then the canal would be full of water like a giant snake, and it would slither toward the river, the ocean, or a larger canal. In its slow gyration, small waves, disturbances on the water's surface, not really waves, might form, and I would train my ear to hear them push the water in the canal along. I'll curl into a ball near the fence that's supposed to block us from jumping in and being carried out to sea or from standing knee-deep and fishing like we used to do in the rivers before they became canals. If it rains, and there's enough water to make waves, then I'll sleep there.

But most of the time, there isn't enough. The rain would need to be heavy that day for the canal to fill enough to surge like a river, and most of the time, it's half-dried by nightfall. The water creeps along in a trickle or moves in a shallow slurry across the bottom of the canal, sure to dry up the next morning when the sun peeks over the horizon. On these nights, I won't sleep. No matter how hard I try. The girl sleeps, and I don't.

Instead, I look for flowers that my daughter insists are there, but I don't see any. Or I do, but I know they are not the one I named her for, so my eyes cloud over, and it's as though they aren't all around, growing through cracks in the pavement or falling in a gentle shower from the trees that surround my estate. I worry I won't recognize the flower, like I sometimes don't recognize my daughter. I worry that I will see the flower and not know that that is my daughter. The girl in me sleeps. Maybe she is my daughter. Maybe when I remember her name and call it out to her, she'll stir from her sleep and look at me.

I see the *kaduk* growing wild in heart shapes all around me. They are stubborn and grow in thickets everywhere I walk. Maybe they hide the flowers behind them. If I haven't eaten that day, I will grab a handful and shove them into my mouth. I can only guess at what they taste like. My tongue is leathery and covered in film, and I no longer taste things as I used to. I can't remember the taste from my younger days either. I just know the *kaduk* is still there. It grows. It remembers to grow. It remembers to be wild when so much else has been forgotten. I want to reconnect with something when I eat it, but I don't know what. When I eat them, I want to remember something, but I don't. I wish I named you Kaduk instead of whatever flower I chose all those years ago. If I had, I would remember your name.

WONG PHUI NAM

After Us

As the year-end monsoon wore on,
its surging waters devoured the land,
leaving into the new year, a kingdom
half drowned in a sea of mud.
Out of this desolation, our houses
rise like islands, offering shelter
to frogs and other small life from the fields,
drawing after them snakes
out of flushed out mud holes in the ground.
Dawn breaks now as a vast silence
over watery mudflats. Birds have fled.
Even egrets heading south from northern winters
no longer stop to fish in our fields
but fly on, crying into darkening thunderheads.

Still, our balding of the mountains goes on
even as their sides shear off
into every season's deluge pouring down the plains,
choking our waterways, wells, and ponds.
Such carnage leaves the plains open to a growing vicious sun.

But the King, he only waits out the season
busies himself with plans for new campaigns,
while having his monks to imbue us with peace
through daily deep incantation of the sacred texts.
At the high stone face, artisans serving his intent
cut his made-up glories onto monuments
raised for a short illusive eternity.
And the people? They too are busy
They have their sowing, and
they have their reaping between floods.
What remains of us here will be told mud—

Of seas dying into miles of sun blighted wastes,
purged of kings, of monks, artisans,
and all that infestation of people,
all else than such life as lizards and scorpions

Not till we let the mountains re-green
will the jungles and small streams come surging back
to a re-awakening to the fullness
of primeval green on the plains
covering a rich, fertile and teeming, sub-arboreal darkness.

After us, life is.

Come Home_____

8 Responses to the Phrase, Go Back to Where You Came from

1.
Oh,
you mean,
Minnesota?

In which case,
here I am.

2.
Oh,
you mean,
where I'm really from.

In which case,
here I am.

3.
If this is in reference
to my people,
then
you are going to have to be
a little bit more specific.
How about trying,
Go back to St. Paul,
or
Go back to Fresno,
Go back to Ban Vinai,
Go back to Long Cheng.

Upon taking my advice,
also realize,
you are not the first
to give the command of
return,
to point us
in the opposite direction
with the barrel of a pistol.
Call me Hmong,
before you call me American
because Hmong is the closest word
I know to home.

4.
Do you ever wonder where you came from?
Do you ever find comfort,
in vague memories of Ellis Island?
How many servings
from the melting pot
did it take for you to arrive
at this conversation?
Maybe,
you take pride in the May Flower.
Maybe,
you are an original American.
Do you ever ask yourself
if the land that you stand on today
once belonged to someone else?
Do you ever ask yourself
if the land
never belonged to any of us
and if instead,
we belonged to the land?

5.
When I was younger,
I made the journey back
to Thailand,
hoping to find
our villages still dotting
the slopes of mountain sides,
hoping to hear
kwv txhiaj
echoing through the valleys.

Upon entering the house of an elder,
he apologizes to me,
embarrassed that his youngest son
could not introduce himself to me in our language,
tells me,
that if you want to grow up
to be anything more than a farmer or a servant
in this country,
you must learn to leave your language behind.
I want to tell him,
that throughout my time here,
I have never felt
so close to where I come from.

6.
My mother tells me,
that before
I ever took in my first breath,
I was an invisible spirit
floating around the clouds
waiting for a stomach
that could paint me pink.
My mother tells me,
death is a slow journey back,
that if not done carefully
our spirit will wander lost
cursing those still living,
but under the watchful eyes
of our loved ones,
we always find our way home.

7.
For most of my life,
I was convinced
that the hummingbird
did not possess a pair of feet
instead always existing
in a state of mid-flight.
How sad,
I thought,
to always be at the mercy of the wind,
to be so close to the earth
yet own none of it.
My time here has taught me

how lucky
the hummingbird is
to belong to the sky.

8.
I am going.
I am going.

Eric Abalajon is currently a lecturer at the University of the Philippines Visayas, Iloilo. His works have appeared in *Cha: An Asian Literary Journal*, *The Tiger Moth Review*, *ANMLY*, *Modern Poetry in Translation*, *Asymptote*, and *Footprints: An Anthology of New Ecopoetry* (Broken Sleep Books, 2022). He lives near Iloilo City.

Ann Ang is an assistant professor of English literature at the National Institute of Education, Nanyang Technological University, Singapore. Her research has been published in the *Journal of Postcolonial Writing*, the *Cambridge Journal of Postcolonial Literary Inquiry*, and *ELH*. Ann's current research interests are transnational and postcolonial writing from Malaysia, Singapore, the Philippines, and India. Ann is also a writer of poetry and fiction, and has edited several anthologies, including *Food Republic* (2020). She is also one of the founding editors of *PR&TA*, a journal of creative praxis in Southeast Asia.

Phương Anh is a translator, writer from Vietnam, and editor at GENCONTROLZ. Their words have found home in magazines and blogs such as *Asymptote*, *PR&TA*, *Interpret Magazine*, *SAND*, and *Modern Poetry in Translation*. At present, they are doing cultural studies at University College London and are a part-time bookseller at Waterstones.

Mark Anthony Angeles is a full-time instructor in the Departamento ng Filipino, College of Education at the University of Santo Tomas. He received his master's degree in Filipino: Malikhaing Pagsulat from the University of the Philippines, Diliman. In 2013, he was a writer-in-residence of the International Writing Program at The University of Iowa, United States. A multi-awarded poet, fictionist, and essayist, his books include *Kuwento ng Dalawang Lungsod*, a Filipino translation of Charles Dickens's *A Tale of Two Cities*, published by the Komisyon sa Wikang Filipino and National Commission for Culture and the Arts in 2018. He is a columnist for *Pinoy Weekly*, the literary editor of bulatlat.com, and features contributor of GMA News Online. In 2021, the University of the Philippines Press released his book *Ang Huling Emotero*, a collection of 144 dagli and a critical paper that delineated the history of the said native form in the country.

Sharmini Aphrodite was born in Kota Kinabalu, Sabah, and raised between the cities of Johor Bahru and Singapore. Her short fiction has been shortlisted for the Commonwealth Short Story Prize, placed on the Australian Book Review Jolley Prize, and appears online and in print. She is a fiction editor for the literary journal *SUSPECT*.

Khairani Barokka is a writer, editor, and artist from Jakarta based in London and is editor of *Modern Poetry in Translation*. Okka's work aims to center disability justice as anticolonial practice, has been presented widely internationally, and has received many commissions and nominations. Among others, she's been a UNFPA Indonesian Young Leader Driving Social Change, a Delfina Foundation Associate Artist, an Associate Artist at the National Centre for Writing, and an *Artforum* Must-See. Her performances include the one-woman show *Eve and Mary Are Having Coffee*; her books include *Stairs and Whispers: D/deaf and Disabled Poets Write Back* (coedited; Nine Arches), *Indigenous Species* (Tilted Axis), *Rope* (Nine Arches), and most recently, *Ultimatum Orangutan* (Nine Arches), shortlisted for the Barbellion Prize. The forthcoming *Annah, Infinite* (Tilted Axis) will be her first creative nonfiction book.

Christian Jil Benitez is a scholar from the Philippines. He teaches at the Ateneo de Manila University, where he earned his AB-MA in Filipino literature. He is currently pursuing his PhD in comparative literature at Chulalongkorn University in Thailand. A prized poet and essayist, his critical and creative works primarily move around the Philippine notion of time, as intuited through the rubrics of the tropical, the poetic, and the (neo)material, and have recently appeared in *eTropic*, *Kritika Kultura*, *Philippine Studies*, and *The Routledge Handbook of Literature and Ecofeminism*, among others. He is the associate editor of the Filipino journal *Katipunan*. His first book, *Isang Dalumat ng Panahon*, was published by ADMU Press.

Alexandra A. Bichara is a PhD Comparative Literature student at the University of the Philippines Diliman. She received her undergraduate degree in Literature (English) from the Ateneo de Manila University in the Philippines and her MA in Literature, Landscape and Environment from Bath Spa University in the United Kingdom. In 2022, she won a Palanca award for her essay, "The Helmsman's Daughter." Her academic interests lie in ecocriticism, ecotrauma, and critical animal studies. She is the proud mom of Furball, her beautiful, sweet kitty son.

Bernard Capinpin is a poet and translator. He received a PEN/Heim Translation Fund Grant for a translation of Edel Garcellano's *A Brief Investigation to a Long Melancholia*. He lives in the Philippines.

F. Jordan Carnice is a writer and visual artist from Bohol, Philippines. His works have appeared in *Sustaining the Archipelago: An Anthology of*

Philippine Ecopoetry, MIDLVLMAG, Anomaly, Sunday Mornings at the River, Quarterly Literary Review Singapore, Voice & Verse Poetry Magazine, and the University of the Philippines Institute of Creative Writing's *Dx Machina: Literature in the Time of COVID-19 Vol. 5*, among several others. He is a recipient of fellowships from national writing workshops in the Philippines, and he has served as a panelist twice in the country's Taboan Writers Festival. He won the poetry grand prize in the 2020 Cebu Climate Emergency Literature and Arts Competition for his poem "There is Too Much Light in This World." He has authored two poetry chapbooks—*Weights & Cushions* (2018) and *How to Make an Accident* (2019)—and he is working on his first full-length book. He can be found online through Instagram (@thebullfrog__ and @art.bullfrog) and Twitter (@thebullfrog__).

Jonathan Chan is a writer and editor of poems and essays. Born in New York to a Malaysian father and South Korean mother, he was raised in Singapore and educated at Cambridge and Yale Universities. He is the author of the poetry collection *Going Home* (Landmark, 2022). He has recently been moved by the work of Noah Arm Choi, Claudia Rankine, and Lorine Niedecker. More of his writing can be found at jonbcy. wordpress.com.

Choo Yi Feng (he/him) is an intertidal explorer, environmental activist, ecologist, and fiction writer. His short stories have been published in *Foglifter Journal, Anathema: Spec from the Margins, Queer Southeast Asia* and *Alluvium*, the journal of Literary Shanghai. He was nominated for the Pushcart Prize in 2022 for his short story, *Spider Hunters*. Yi Feng dwells, spiritually, metaphorically, and physically, at tropical coastlines, mudflats, and coral rubble. He is interested in exploring the more-than-human forces that coproduce shorelines as sites that are at once azure, touristic, scummy, pungent, profitable, and unruly, as well as the multivalent possibilities of exuberance, care, mourning, and witnessing to be found here. At present, he spends his spare time between movement work with the Singapore Climate Rally and writing his debut novel, *Brack*.

Rina Garcia Chua (she/her/siya) is a creative and critical scholar from the Philippines who is currently based in the unceded tṁxʷúlaʔxʷ of the syilx / Okanagan peoples. She has been a 2022–2023 Jack and Doris Shadbolt Fellow in the Humanities at Simon Fraser University, a 2023 Affective Currents Institute Fellow at Dartmouth College, and she received her PhD from The University of British Columbia. Rina is the editor of *Sustaining the Archipelago: An Anthology of Philippine Ecopoetry* (UST Publishing House, 2018) and coeditor of *Empire and Environment: Ecological Ruin in the Transpacific* (University of Michigan Press, 2022). Her current book manuscript develops the framework of a migrant reading practice in analyzing curations, collations, and anthologies of literary and visual cultures, and she is completing her poetry collection, *A Geography of (Un)Natural Hazards*, which is a visual and poetic response to migrant and arrivant cultures, liminal environments, and violences of form and language. Her website is http://rinagarciachua.com.

Teresa Mei Chuc was born in Sài Gòn, Việt Nam, and fled her Vietnamese homeland with her mother and brother shortly after the American war in Việt Nam, spending three and a half months in a freight boat stranded in the South China Sea before being rescued. Her father, who had served in the Army of the Republic of Việt Nam, remained in a Việt Cộng re-education prison camp for nine years. Altadena Poet Laureate, Editor-in-Chief (2018–2020), and a member of the Pasadena Rose Poets, Teresa Mei Chuc is the author of three full-length collections of poetry, *Invisible Light* (Many Voices Press, 2018), *Keeper of the Winds* (FootHills Publishing, 2014), and *Red Thread* (Fithian Press, 2012). Teresa's new poetry chapbook, *Incidental Takes*, is forthcoming from Hummingbird Press in 2023. Teresa teaches literature and writing at a public high school in Los Angeles.

feby's poetry and work intersect themes of eco-phenomenology, anti-capitalism, and feminism. In particular, she is interested in dissolving the structure and conditions of capitalism that reduce the Earth and humans as commodities. Her teachers include Thich Nhat Hanh, the body, her communities, and Data from Star Trek. She is also a part of a Balinese performing arts and gamelan ensemble, Gamelan Sekar Jaya, based in Berkeley, CA. She draws inspiration from her ancestral land in Indonesia. She is based in the Bay Area, on the unceded territory of Huichin.

Natalie Foo Mei-Yi is a writer by profession. After studying literature, film, and philosophy at university, she embarked on an eclectic series of jobs as a film reviewer, a police intelligence officer, a barmaid, a creative copywriter, an architectural magazine editor, the writer-editor at a performing arts center, and an arts writer. Now, she writes for a living and makes poetry and art in private, surrounded by kiddy clutter, 80s and 90s cassettes, sci-fi DVDs, a lifetime collection of books, and a hoard of collected shells, rocks, and twigs.

Fahrunnisa Hidayat (aka Annisa Hidayat) was born in Taliwang, West Sumbawa, Indonesia, on May 29, 1988. She is a poet, editor, and independent researcher. She continued her master's degree at the Department of Languages & Cultures of Southeast Asia, Asia Africa Institute, University of Hamburg, Germany. Her first book of poetry, *Menuju Laut Utara* (Heading the North Sea), which contained her travel notes during her two-year stay in North Germany (2017–2019), was published in 2021 by the literary community Akarpohon. Her poems have been published in an anthology of women of Lombok Island, *Taman Pitanggang* (Pitanggang Garden, 2014), and *Perempuan Langit 3* (The Sky Woman, 2017). Her writings have been published in several online media and print newspapers, mostly about travel and traditional cultures. As a freelance researcher, she manages her own website, "Balawas Heritage," balawas.id, an ethnographic medium that focuses on literature, heritage, and culture.

Chrystal Ho is a writer from Singapore who works with poetry and nonfiction. Her writing has previously been published in *The Tiger Moth Review*, *PR&TA Journal*, and *The Hawker*, among others. A former Global Writing & Speaking Fellow at NYU Shanghai, she is currently a Creative Resident at the National Library Board.

Ian Nievero Jerez finished his degree in AB Literature at the University of Santo Tomas in 2019. He is currently taking MFA Creative Writing at De La Salle University, Manila. He has been teaching literature for four years at the Junior High School of Mont Michel School in Quezon City. He was a literary writer at The Flame (the Official Student Publication of the UST Faculty of Arts and Letters) and served as the assistant editor for Prose for Dapitan: Insureksiyon, the 2019 Literary Folio of the same publication.

Gabriela Lee teaches creative writing and children's literature at the Department of English & Comparative Literature at the University of the Philippines. Her prose has been published in the Philippines, the United States, Canada, and Norway, most recently in the anthology *Unquiet Spirits: Essays by Asian Women in Horror*, edited by Lee Murray and Angela Yuriko Smith. She has received a National Children's Book Award citation in the Philippines for her children's book, *Cely's Crocodile: The Story and Art of Araceli Limcaco-Dans*. Her latest short story collection, *A Playlist for the End of the World*, was published by the University of the Philippines Press. She is currently pursuing a PhD in the English Department at the University of Pittsburgh. You can learn more about her work at www.sundialgirl.com.

Setu Legi was born in Yogyakarta and raised by parents who were teachers and traditional traders. He completed his studies in the Faculty of Art and Design at the Indonesian Institute of Art (ISI) in Yogyakarta in 2000. Alongside the inflammation of the sociopolitical situation in Indonesia in 1998, he and his friends established the Taring Padi art and cultural community. He is now more focused on his work as an individual while collaborating with artists in other fields. A number of group exhibitions he has been involved in include ID—Contemporary Art Indonesia, Germany (2010–2011), Biennale Jogja XI—Equator #1, Shadow Lines Indonesia meets India (2011), and Climate Art Festival "Hutan di titik Nol" (2013). He has had several solo shows, including Black Lights—Yogyakarta (2005), Social

Realities—Germany (2005), Are You Ready—interactive mixed media, and Yogyakarta (2008).

Pamela Ng's interdisciplinary interest lies in the nexus of nature and the arts. With a keen eye and ear for the intricacies of the environment, she seeks to communicate the value of biodiversity conservation and human–wildlife coexistence through unique storytelling, visuals, and soundscapes. In all her encounters with wildlife, she strives to renew, reconnect, and reframe people's relationships with their environment and biodiversity within. Professionally, Pam works at a consultancy firm, enhancing business resilience through climate and sustainability risk advisory. Apart from work, she takes the time to conduct immersive and experiential nature programs with Untamed Paths and actively volunteers with ACRES as a Wildlife Rescue officer. She received her Masters in Biodiversity Conservation and Nature-Based Climate Solutions from the National University of Singapore and a Bachelor of Fine Arts in Visual Communications from the School of Art, Design and Media (ADM) in Nanyang Technological University.

Enbah Nilah is an educator and poet-in-progress. Her interest lies in the "almost(s)" and "not-quite(s)," the gray-in-between regions of unbelonging. Her works can also be found in *Adi Magazine* (NY), *Persephone's Daughters* literary magazine (NZ), the *Dirty Thirty Anthology* (AUS), and *When I Say Spoken, You Say Word* (MY).

Carmie Ortego is a native of Talalora, Samar. At present, she is the HUMSS Coordinator at National University—MOA Senior High School in Pasay City. Her poems and essays have appeared in *Kabisdak*, SunStar Cebu, *Katitikan*, *Kill Your Darlings*, *Likhaan 16*, and are featured in Anvil's and DIWA's textbooks on Creative Nonfiction and 21st Century Literature, respectively. She was part of the Filipino delegation for the Bersong EuroPinoy 2021, a program of the European Union delegation in the Philippines.

Diana Rahim is currently a community worker, writer, and occasional visual artist. She serves as an editor for *Beyond the Hijab*, an online platform sharing the narratives and critical perspectives of Muslim women in Singapore. Her central concerns in her creative work have been the politics of public space, the experience of the environment, feminism, and class. Most recently, her fiction has been anthologized in *Singa-pura-pura: Malay Speculative Fiction from Singapore* and *Best New Singaporean Short Stories: Volume Five*. Her essay has also been anthologized in *Making Kin: Ecofeminist Essays from Singapore*. When she's not working or busy surviving, she likes to read, love her cats, and dream of autonomous futures.

Serina Rahman is a Southeast Asian Studies Department (NUS) lecturer, teaching environmental politics; religion, magic, and society; and about Southeast Asia by sea. Trained as a conservation scientist, her practice is community empowerment through citizen science, community research and ecotourism, and artisanal fisheries resource management, all of which is done at Kelab Alami, a community organization in Johor, Malaysia, that she cofounded in 2008. Her research also includes (un)sustainable development, Malaysian rural politics, and political ecology. Serina is an Iskandar Malaysia Social Hero Award Winner for Environmental Protection (2014) and was highlighted as a Channel News Asia Climate Warrior in 2021. In another lifetime, she was once a mermaid but is now trying to make the most of a sentence as a human living among fishermen in southwest Johor, Malaysia, where she does most of her research, community practice, and writing. The sea is her lifeline.

Mohamed Shaker is a Singaporean writer based in Singapore. He holds an MA in creative writing from LaSalle College of the Arts. His writing has been published in *PR&TA* journal and *The Best Asian Short Stories 2022*. Currently an educator, his writing explores how Singapore and Singaporeans continue to live with and in their past in the present.

Jacqueline Shea is a poet and Ph.D. student studying comparative culture and language, specializing in sociocultural linguistics with a secondary focus on affinity studies. She earned her MA from Arizona State University in Spanish, and she also holds an undergraduate degree in sustainability. She currently teaches undergraduate Spanish courses while researching the relationship between language and culture, emotions, folktales, and psychology from a cross-cultural perspective. Her goal is to foster greater empathy between different cultures and species through better understanding how they connect within the contexts of linguistic and cultural productions.

Cat T. is a Malaysian speculative fiction writer with a focus on fabulism and horror within their local contexts. Cat has works featured in Night Sky Press, The B'K, Strange Horizons, and was a finalist for Dream Foundry's Writing Contest 2021. More can be found at https://thecatwriter.carrd.co/.

Esther Vincent Xueming is the Editor-in-Chief and founder of *The Tiger Moth Review*, an independent eco journal of art and literature based in Singapore. She is the author of *Red Earth* (Blue Cactus Press; Pagesetters, 2021), an ecofeminist collection of poetry. She is coeditor of *Making Kin: Ecofeminist Essays from Singapore* (Ethos Books, 2021), *Poetry Moves* (Ethos Books, 2020), and *Little Things* (Ethos Books, 2013), and was invited to be a guest regional editor (Asia) for a special eco-themed issue of *The Global South* (University of Mississippi). Her essays on ecopoetry, ecofeminism, ecospirituality, and ecowriting and healing have been published in *The Trumpeter, EcoTheo Review, Sinking City Review*, and *Quarterly Literary Review Singapore*.

Wong Phui Nam (1935–2022) was a Malaysian poet and one of the pioneers of Malaysian writing in the English language. In the 1950s, he was actively involved in *The New Cauldron* and later as the editor of *Litmus One* and *30 Poems* at Raffles College (which later became the University of Malaya, now the National University of Singapore). He also published an apprentice work, *Toccata on Ochre Sheaves*. His poems in the 1960s appeared in *Bunga Emas* and were then collated in what many consider his seminal work, *How the Hills Are Distant*, in 1968. Following a hiatus of thirty years, Wong Phui Nam published *Remembering Grandma and Other Rumours* in 1989, *Ways of Exile* in 1993, *Against the Wilderness* in 2000, *An Acre of Day's Glass* in 2005, and *The Hidden Papyrus of Hen-taui* in 2013 (republished in 2018). His final posthumous collection, *In the Mirror*, is being edited by Brandon K. Liew and Daryl Lim Wei Jie.

Kevin Yang is a Hmong American spoken word artist and documentary filmmaker from the Twin Cities, Minnesota. Kevin works at Twin Cities PBS, where he connects educators to media resources. Kevin represented Minnesota at the BlackBerryPeach National Poetry Slam in 2022 and represented Hamline University at the College Union Poetry Slam Invitational in 2012 and 2014. Kevin's work has been published on platforms such as *Button Poetry* and in the anthology, *We Are Meant to Rise*.

Alvin Yapan is currently the editor of the journal *Katipunan: Journal of Research in Filipino Language, Literature, Arts and Culture*. He is an associate professor at the Department of Filipino, Ateneo de Manila University. He has a forthcoming book about his research on folk aesthetics, *Ang Bisa ng Pag-uulit sa Katutubong Panitikan* (*The Efficacy of Repetition in Folk Literature*).

A former news anchor, broadcast journalist, columnist, and communications officer for a conservation organization, **Christina Yin** is now a writer and senior lecturer at Swinburne University of Technology, Sarawak Campus. Christina's PhD thesis, *Creative Nonfiction: True Stories of People involved in Fifty Years of Conservation of the Orang-utan in Sarawak, Malaysia*, combined her two passions: creative nonfiction and conservation. She lives in Sarawak, Malaysian Borneo, with her husband and two children.